I0594137

HIS BUXOM BEAUTY

KAPOW SERIES, BOOK #2

RENÉE DAHLIA

HIS BUXOM BEAUTY

RENÉE DAHLIA

Image is everything, or is it?

Advertising executive STU COOPER is fascinated by his hairdresser. Over the past two years, he has trusted her with his biggest secret – that his silver highlights are faked to give him a look of seniority in business. He adores her cheerful creative outlook on life, and for too long he has tried to ignore that she has the best boobs in town. If only he could reconcile his interest in her with his overwhelming need to live up to the image he has spent years cultivating.

Hairdresser POPPY KARAHALIOS has inherited her grandfather's barber shop in trendy Surry Hills. With her creative flair, she'd love to take the salon into modernity but family loyalty holds her back. One client makes all the hard work running her own business worthwhile. For two years, she's been tinting the edges of his temples with grey, using all her skills to make him the most desirable fake silver fox in town. For two years, she has contented herself with fantasy, and those tingly touches against his skin as she worked. Because Poppy knows for certain that someone so concerned with his image wouldn't be interested in an overweight hairdresser with rainbow hair.

ABOUT THE AUTHOR

Renée Dahlia is an unabashed romance reader who loves feisty women and strong, clever men. Her books reflect this, with a side note of awkward humour. Renée has a science degree in physics. When not distracted by the characters fighting for attention in her brain, she works in the horse-racing industry doing data analysis and writing magazine articles. When she isn't reading or writing, Renée spends her time with her partner and four children, volunteers on the local cricket club committee, and is the Secretary of Romance Writers Australia.

ACKNOWLEDGMENTS

I acknowledge the Wangal people of the Eora Nation, the traditional owners of the land this work was produced on. I pay my respects to Elders past and present.

For everyone who strives for success, whatever that might look like.

1

_____

"What's on the schedule today?" Poppy asked her apprentice, Levi, even though she knew. She'd taken the phone call yesterday listening to Stu's baritone warm against her ear even though he said nothing interesting. Only a confirmation of his appointment time.

"Just the usual, a bunch of old blokes wanting short, back and sides. Oh, and 'Stu, call me Stu' will be in at ten for a touch up." Levi smirked at the mention of their hottest client. They'd often gossiped about him, and his ultra-hot body.

"He's not gay, you know." Poppy winked at her apprentice. She hoped the blasé joke would cover her blush.

Levi waved a copy of the latest society pages from the paper where Stu was photographed next to some beautiful thin model woman. "Might be bi!"

"True. I guess you can always hope."

Levi grinned. "With that arse, it'd be a shame if he was straight." Levi commented continually on the breadth of

Stu's shoulders, and his gorgeous arse, to the extent that he'd started a Stu's Arse Appreciation Society, and whispered SAAS every time Stu left the shop. Poppy was a fully paid up member of SAAS, but she didn't dare mention her fantasies. She'd give her favourite scissors away if she could see Stu, naked and spreadeagled on her bed, his hands and feet tied to corner posts, and his cock hard and erect for her. She just knew, or perhaps it was a pointless wish, that he'd have a gorgeous cock. Not too big as to be ridiculous, but big enough and broad enough for a hot ride. She'd lick his body, taste him as he strained against her silky ties, tease him until he cursed her. Until he begged for her, and only then would she touch his cock.

"Poppy…"

"Yeah." She blinked away the fantasy, tried not to fan her face, as Levi called her name.

"Time to open up for the day."

"Right." She nodded, blowing out a long breath. Stu would be here a little over an hour, sitting in her chair with that relaxed charm he had. She glanced in one of the mirrors to ensure she was presentable, saw the pink flush on her skin, and walked to the front door to unlock it. Time for business. Spiro's Barber Shop, since 1949, as the sign on the shop in trendy Surry Hills proudly proclaimed. After an apprenticeship with the highly vaunted Jean-Phillipe, international opportunities had beckoned. Her ambitions had stalled when Pappous' arthritis had become too much for him, and she'd taken over Spiro's. It had been another apprenticeship of sorts, having to satisfy Pappous that she could run his business without upsetting his view of how it should be, as well as learning accounting, and all those other skills required to run a small business. Pappous had died just over two years ago and had gifted her the business in his will. Some of the family weren't happy with his decision, mostly because she'd also gained the valuable real estate that went with it. Poppy thought they could keep their opinions to themselves, especially since they'd got other properties of his, without the heartache of employing people, and trying to make enough money for food every month. Renting out the top floor of the building was the only way she actually turned a profit, not that she'd admit that to any of her large clan. If only she could take this business into the modern world and get the clients she really wanted. The ones who would happily spend hundreds to sit in her chair for a couple of hours for the sake of her art, not the ones who wanted a cheap as chips simple buzz cut.

She flicked the sign on the window over, and pulled the door open, shoving a wedge under it to keep it there. The luxurious warm spring air drifted inside. October had to be one of the nicest times of year in Sydney, with winter most definitely over, and the heat of summer starting to strengthen. Jacaranda blossoms showered the footpath with purple flowers. She hoisted the blackboard sign with the list of their current specials and glanced over the little ditty Levi had written on it. No typos, nothing too cheap, she nodded, all good. She set the sign in its usual spot outside the window and went inside to start the day's typical boring work. Her toes tapped impatiently in her shoe.

"Do you want a coffee before our first client arrives?" Poppy asked her apprentice. Any excuse to get out for a bit, away from the suffocating boredom of Pappous' clients. Something had to change soon. Two years of this drudgery with her dreams put on hold. When she'd taken over, the first year had been a blur, working out how to make money, dealing with her grief on losing her grandfather and mentor, and balancing all the family's opinions. She felt like she was finally finding her feet as a business owner, and now her dreams of a fashionable salon had started to seep back into her life. Teasing her, just as Stu inadvertently teased her by being her only client who demanded technical perfection. His glorious good looks and charming smile only added to his unattainableness.

Levi flicked his long fringe back. "Like a real one? Yes, please."

"Yes, a real one. I'll shout." Poppy grabbed her purse from under the counter and paced out of the shop. "Good morning, Con." She nodded to the morning's first client as she walked down the footpath to the café only three doors down. Normally, her and Levi made do with instant from the little kitchenette out the back next to the storeroom, and she tried not to be tempted by the smell of baked goods and real coffee from down the street.

She swallowed as she entered the café. What was wrong with her? She had her dream job, and her own shop. Where had this frustration with her life come from? Levi would be no use to talk to about it. He was her apprentice for a start, so it'd be weird to talk to him about this, and besides, he'd just say she needed some good sex; which brought the image of Stu naked on her bed roaring back to life. Fuck. Levi was probably right. Maybe she'd have a double shot and call some friends to go out tonight. Time to scratch an itch, it'd been too long since she'd had sex with anyone. It all came back to Spiros—she had no time for dating anymore, no time for leisure or pleasure, not with a business to keep afloat.

"Two double shot flat whites, thanks." She dug around in her purse for some cash.

"Anything else?"

Poppy shook her head, clenching her teeth to stop her blurting out a comment about the dreadful dye job someone had given the poor young woman serving. Poppy slid the cash on the counter and stared at her boring shoes instead. Ogling Stu might be aiming way too high, but she could find someone tonight to have a good time with, to let her push all the weight of her business aside for a few hours of entertainment. She straightened and stared at the girl's hair, unable to stop herself assessing it.

"Here you go."

"Thanks. By the way—" Poppy couldn't help it. "Where did you get your hair done?"

"A Cut Above. Do you like it?" The young lady flicked her head. No, it's crooked and the dye is already fading. Poppy couldn't believe that she'd paid for that atrocity.

"It's just that it's started to fade, so I was wondering if you wanted to drop by my salon to get it touched up." Poppy paused, trying to keep her chin high. She hated asking for business, but she hated seeing a bad job just as much. Her fingers twitched with the need to fix it.

The young woman tugged at her hair, staring at it. "Oh

my god, you are right. Those assholes. I only had it done two weeks ago."

"It should last much longer than that." Talking about hair came easily, and Poppy's nerves disappeared.

"Yeah, it should. Where is your place? I might drop by."

"Spiro's Barber Shop. Don't mind the name, we do heaps more than old guy haircuts. I'm fully trained as a colourist." Poppy heard the defensive panic in her voice as the young woman's eyes shifted sideways.

"Ok. Yeah, maybe, I'll think about it." *Yeah, sure. You and everyone else who I want as a client.* Poppy grabbed the two coffees. "Whenever you are ready. I promise I'll fix that for you." She turned on her heels and rushed out before she could hear the inevitable laughter.

2

———

Stu glanced up and down the street before he walked into Spiro's Barber Shop. He loved this little shop. It was perfectly located, only a short walk from the office. The old-fashioned exterior hid the genius who worked inside. She'd kept his secret for two years, meeting him every few weeks to touch up the fake grey at his temples. He still remembered the day when the boss of Westfield had told him they couldn't do business with someone so young and inexperienced. Being in advertising, he knew it all came down to perception. The perfect solution had come thanks to a joke a colleague told him.

"What four qualifications do you need to become a board member?"

"Male, pale, stale and frail."

Stu decided to get fake silver highlights to give him gravitas, a few grey hairs to make the grey-headed old men of business want to deal with him. Finding Poppy and Spiro's had been a completely fluke, the tiny words at the bottom of the blackboard sign 'specialist in colour treatments' had pulled him in. And Poppy had kept him coming back. Not only was she a genius with hair, she had the best boobs in all of Sydney. Those lush breasts, always hidden under a practical shirt as she worked, with her full hips and round stomach always made his mouth water. She was a true Rubenesque beauty, and he craved her.

Normally, in this situation, he'd paint on a smile, and ask her out. He'd never had any trouble asking other women out on dates. There was something about Poppy which added a certain magnitude to the question. She mattered more than usual; he didn't want her to say no, but after seeing his workmate Ella find happiness with Joey, he knew he wanted the same thing for himself. Poppy was a constant in his life; and he found himself unusually torn between wanting her and not wanting to ruin their current arrangement.

Today, his smile came naturally as he walked in the door and saw Poppy flicking a brush over some old guy's neck, little pieces of hair brushed away as she finished. Her apprentice raked him with his gaze. Every time. It would have amused him, if only he didn't crave for Poppy to do the same. She treated him exactly the same as every other person who walked in here, as if only his hair existed. Every touch, every stroke of her fingers, taunted him until he wanted to beg for a kiss. He wouldn't stoop to that, she had to be keen, because he'd never kissed someone unwilling, and fuck it, he wouldn't start now. If she could be professional, so could he, no matter the personal toll.

Two weeks ago, after his last appointment, her touches, gentle strokes on his temple, her body in close proximity to his, had spurred his vivid imagination until he pictured her as a nude, in oils, stretched out for him, with soft fabric curled around her legs. He'd walked out of there, jaw clenched, and into the café nearby to jerk off in the toilet. Ridiculous. He'd tried to wash her out of his brain by going out to prowl Sydney's nightlife. Every evening for two weeks, he'd bought drinks for a different woman, all of them curvy and confident. Poppy substitutes, but none of them were her. For two weeks, he'd gone home alone to wank. This had to end today.

She smiled. "Hey Stu, same again today?" Her sultry voice slid over his skin as he slipped into her chair. He stared into the mirror, directly into her round brown eyes, as she stroked his head. She probably did this to everyone, this exploration of his scalp with her fingers. Did everyone get this electric zing from every touch? His chest expanded as he held her gaze. He tried to will her fingers into shifting lower, ideally around his cock, but he'd make do with anything. Goddamn it, he was desperate for her touch. For two years, he'd longed for more. Those soft curves pressed against him, her skin against his.

"No, not the same."

Her mouth pursed into a perfectly kissable o, and he held his breath.

"It's time to change this—" He referred to them, not his haircut.

"You want to get rid of the grey, or expand it, so it looks like natural aging?" she asked, missing his point.

"Come to lunch with me. The hair can wait." His planned finesse abandoned him. His strategy was to wait till after his hair was done, when he wouldn't be distracted by his reactions to her touch. She tilted her head and stared back at him.

"Hair should never wait." Little spots of pink appeared on her cheeks, and her nostrils flared slightly. Perhaps she wasn't as unaffected as he'd assumed. Or maybe she was annoyed at his dismissal. Hair mattered to her, so he would wait another hour. In the context of two long years, and with her fingers toying with his locks, he'd survive. Each stroke added to the anticipation.

He waved his hand. "Do the hair, as usual, then come to lunch with me. That guy can watch the place for an hour."

"That guy... You mean, Levi, my apprentice?"

"Yes. Levi looks capable."

"He is. A little more notice might have been good, though." Surely, she wasn't going to say no. She sounded faintly annoyed at his presumption.

"Be flexible."

"Says the executive in expensive shirts who fakes his age. I'm sure you have all the time in the world for lunches. I don't." Her usual happy charm disappeared into snark, and he loved it. A perverse reaction, her sarcasm making the chase more exciting.

"Make time."

"For you?" Her eyebrows lifted at his command.

"It's fine, Poppy, I can mind the shop. Enjoy lunch with Stu." The apprentice called out. *Thank you, Levi.* He'd send the guy a carton of beer later, an appreciation gift, if this worked out.

"See, Levi can hold the fort. Come to lunch with me."

Her fingers tightened on his skull and she chewed on her bottom lip. Her kissable bottom lip, a dusky rose, firing up the possibility of her nipples. Would they be the same colour, or darker?

"Maybe. I'll have to look at the schedule. Now let's get this hair touched up."

Stu forced his brain to wander away during his appointment. Experience taught him plenty of stratagems to survive his head being massaged by Poppy's proficient fingers. He flicked through a magazine, tried not to flinch when her body brushed the back of his neck at one point. Anticipation built into tension in his shoulders until the final blow dry. The touch-ups to keep his black hair grey all the way to the roots was a finnicky process. If it hadn't brought him multiple new large clients, or the constant proximity to Poppy, he wouldn't have bothered with the fuss. Poppy made the fuss worthwhile.

"That should keep you going for another few weeks," she said eventually. She turned away, putting equipment into a trolley beside her. Every movement of hers was efficient, practiced, competent. She waved him towards the front of the shop, then picked up a broom and quickly swept around where he'd been sitting. Pride infused her actions. It had always been one of his favourite parts of his appointments with her, not just that she always delivered him perfect hair, but the way she obviously adored her job. She disappeared through the door at the back of the shop. Stu stared at the closed door until a cough made him turn away to see Levi standing by the little front desk.

"Here you go. Keep the change and get yourself a drink tonight. Thanks for covering for Poppy." Stu kept his voice low, so only Levi could hear, even though Poppy wasn't in the room.

Levi nodded and took the money. "She's a good boss. She deserves to the be treated properly. Be sure you do that."

Stu's respect for the young apprentice grew in spades. "I will."

"Are you sure you'll be alright covering for me, Levi?" Poppy joined their group.

"Yes, go on with you. Have fun." The apprentice nudged her shoulder and grinned. He made an odd hissing noise. Poppy flushed as she laughed at him.

"SAAS yourself." Her comment made no sense, perhaps some sort of hairdresser code. Stu shook his head and gestured to the front door of the shop.

"Shall we?"

"Yes. I'll be back soon, Levi." Poppy hovered, her concern for the apprentice obvious.

"I'll be fine. There is nothing in the books, and we hardly ever have a walk in on a Thursday lunchtime."

Poppy sighed, a resigned noise, hardly the sound Stu wanted to inspire in her.

He placed his hand on the small of her back. "Come on." Touching her was a strategic mistake. Heat raced up his arm and punched him in the chest. His heart sped up, especially when she didn't pull away. She moved with him towards the door and let him guide her through.

As soon as they started walking along the pavement, she put space between them.

"Where are we going?"

"I thought this little place would do. It's close enough for you to rush back and save Levi if you need." Stu made up his mind quickly, figuring that would ease her concerns about the apprentice. Perhaps she felt responsibility for him, she was obviously the more experienced hairdresser of the two. And he'd never seen the illusive Spiro during any of his visits.

"Sure." She entered the shop, ducking her head away from the waitress with bright pink hair. Stu selected a table and waved for her to sit. She chose to sit with her back to the counter, making him frown.

"Is there a problem?"

"No." She grimaced ruefully. "Kind of. It's awkward."

"And?"

"I bought coffee here this morning and told the waitress that her hair needed a touch up." Poppy's cheeks were flushed again, and she stared down at the menu.

"She should come and see you."

"That's what I said." She glanced up and a smile darted over her lips, quickly disappearing, before she ducked her head down again.

"So, what's the problem?"

"I don't know. I don't think she liked the idea." Poppy's gaze stayed low and she picked at the napkin.

"You what I find helps when I get stuck in an awkward situation like this?"

"What?"

"Be brazen. Your hair is better than hers, you have the whole rainbow, she only has pink." Stu's pulse skipped a beat as Poppy stared at him. He'd hoped she would smile.

"Faded pink that desperately needs help." Poppy's whisper was so quiet, it almost faded away to nothing.

"Hold on. You really care about her hair." He'd assumed it was awkward because the waitress had rejected her services, not because Poppy felt empathy for the poor girl's apparently bad haircut. He couldn't see what was wrong with it, aside from the lurid colour. Funny how Poppy's rainbow hair made him smile, yet others with vibrant colours often looked out of place to him. To be fair to everyone else, Poppy could probably do anything with her hair, even shave it completely off, and he'd still anticipate her touch.

"It doesn't matter. Why did you ask me to lunch?" She shook her head, as if to dismiss her concerns about the wait-ress. He'd asked because he couldn't stop thinking about her. He wanted to undress her and spend an inordinate amount of time caressing her soft curves. She waited, her gaze fixed on his, with those wide brown eyes soaking in every detail of his face. His comment caught in his throat under all her attention.

"Or shall we just sit here in weird silence?" Poppy whispered.

He cleared away the burr in his throat. "The reason I asked you here today—" Stu paused as her finely arched brows lifted, "—is, well, I've been wanting to ask you out on a date."

She frowned, confusion creating wrinkles across her forehead. "Me?"

"Yes." Stu couldn't understand why she seemed so confused. It was a straightforward offer.

3

_____

"**M**e? And after all this time?" Poppy's cynical tone and the snide look in her eyes screamed at him, even though she kept her voice low. Shit. Not the response he'd hoped for. He'd strategized this as the best option to get her to talk to him on his turf. So much for assuming she'd be pleased to be asked.

He cleared his throat. "Yes, after all this time." He stopped himself saying something really daft, like 'it's taken me that long to notice you'; which was a lie, anyway. It'd taken him this long to realise that what he really wanted had been under his nose the whole time. "Look, you can say no." *Don't say no.* His voice cracked.

"To a date? Why are you asking me?" The rosy spots of pink on her cheeks darkened. Fuck. He kept shovelling, unwittingly making the hole bigger. This wasn't going anything like he'd imagined. He'd assumed she also felt the chemistry between them. His gaze dropped to her breasts, and he hauled it back up again. Her curves were a huge part of her appeal, he wanted to bury himself in her, perfectly round and womanly. He'd be lying if he said it wasn't part of his attraction to her, it just wasn't that simplistic.

"Umm, well…" Don't think about her gorgeous plump body. Don't think about sinking into her curves. Think about her competent fingers, her enthusiasm for her job, the way she listened to each of her clients as though they were the only person in the world.

"I'm not exactly your type, or is it just the big boobs you want?" Her nostrils flared, and his face burned. She'd obviously noticed the direction of his glance, and she hunched her shoulders slightly. Bloody hell. He blinked.

"No thanks. Maybe you need a new hairdresser." She started to stand.

"Wait, wait. Please." He pleaded, and she sat down again, one eyebrow arched up. His pulse hammered. This hadn't precisely gone as he'd imagined. Silence hovered, uneasy, between them as he rubbed the back of his neck. He was a star at work, able to convince people to listen to him. This shouldn't be this awkward.

"Obviously I haven't explained this very well. I didn't mean to insult you, Poppy." Pink washed over her cheeks as he used her name, and she crossed her arms. Don't look down. Don't look at the way her breasts spill so deliciously. There was only one option. He had to confess.

"Poppy, I think you are fucking hot, all of you. It's not as simple as saying I have a thing for curvy women and you fit the bill. I love your competence, and the way you make everyone feel comfortable. You've always made me feel welcome in your shop, and your fingers are magic. I've been wanting to ask you out for ages. Please say yes." He sipped some water, his hand shaking a little as he lifted the cup to his dry lips. He couldn't look at her as sweat broke out under his arms.

"What? Me?"

He put the cup down and stared at her. "Yes." How could she not see it? Had she not noticed that his hair appointments had gone from once a month when he first started, to once a week in the last six months. The two week gap between today and his previous appointment had been too long, and was completely his choice because he'd finally realised that his obsession was about more than his own selfish image. He craved being near her, the way her fingers pressed against his scalp, the glimpses of her skin he got in the mirror as she worked behind him. The way her tongue rested at the edge of her luscious mouth whenever she needed to concentrate. And more than that, her happy personality, always chatting to him, and the way she listened to him making feel like he was only person in the world that mattered. He always had his best ideas after his appointments with her. It had taken him ages, too long, to figure out that connection, and then two weeks ago, her breasts had brushed, accidentally, against the back of his neck. Sparks had spun across his flesh and he'd made his decision. If he'd been tormented by dreams of her before that, they were nothing like the desire currently torturing him.

"Bullshit." She drew out the last syllable in cautious wonderment, the previous cynicism in her voice fading. "You said it yourself, you have a thing for curvy women. I'm fat. And you are—" She licked her lips.

"I'm just Stu, and I really want to kiss you." He may as well go all in now that he'd started this. Her eyes darted around the room. He swallowed, ready to plead his case further when she smiled. A slow hesitant smile which grew into a broad relaxed smile making his heart leap with hope.

"A kiss?" She tilted her head a little. "I might just say yes to a kiss, but you are going to have to work for it." Her eyes softened, with the harsh sarcasm at the start of the conversation gone.

"Anything." He leaned forward on his elbows.

"Careful. You are starting to sound desperate." She laughed, her brown eyes dancing as if she suddenly realised the power she had over him. If she only knew how much he wanted to bury his face in her breasts, all that soft flesh to play with. He wanted to fuck her breasts, to come on her throat. God, it was more than that though. There were any number of willing women in Sydney with big tits, and although his thoughts ended up there with ridiculous frequency, he wanted Poppy, not just anyone. He craved Poppy's smile, her attention, and her charm.

"I remember the first time I saw you. You stood alone inside Spiro's, leaning on a broom as I walked in the door. You had red hair that day, a vibrant red that shone like the sun, and you reminded me of Gentileschi's Penitent Magdalene."

"Of what?"

"It's a painting from the Baroque period." In his mind, it explained everything. The Rubenesque plump woman with red hair, seated on a chair in a golden dress. His ideal beauty captured in oils.

"Right… I'll take you word for it." She tucked a bright blue strand behind her ear, "and that's why you want to kiss me?"

"Because when I explained what I wanted with my hair on that first day, I saw something in your eyes. I'd expected laughter or dismissal, but you looked hungry. Like I'd just given you a gift. And I want to inspire that gaze again and again." Preferably with kisses, or more. He definitely wanted more than kisses.

She grinned, biting her bottom lip as her face lit up. "I remember that conversation. For the first time in for-fuck-ing-ever, I had a challenge. What you asked for was so technically difficult—a fake silver fox—I couldn't say yes fast enough."

"What can I do to make you say yes to a kiss?"

"Stu. I don't want a pity kiss from you, just because I am the caretaker of your big secret…"

"How did you know it's a secret?"

"How could I not? You came to my salon and asked, no, scratch that… You whispered your requirement with sunglasses on and wearing a terrible ill-fitting suit. It was obvious you were either an insane creative, or in disguise."

"It's never been pity, Poppy. You see me. That's why I want a kiss. Because you are fucking hot, and you seem to care about me." His heart thumped in his chest, his breath rapid and shallow. Women chased him, he didn't need to ask. This 'asking' process was agony. *Please say yes, Poppy.* He didn't want to beg. The tables had turned on him, and he didn't know how to go forward. An idea floated by and he grinned to himself.

"Don't answer yet." He stood up and walked to the waitress. "Hey there, what do you think of my haircut?" Stu turned his head left and right.

"I don't know, it's nice." The waitress looked at him as if he'd completely lost the plot. He could feel Poppy's stare prickling on his back.

"You see Poppy?" He nodded in her direction. "She's a genius with hair. Don't worry about the old-fashioned look of Spiro's. Poppy works there, and if she says she can fix your hair, you should trust her. She's awesome." Stu gave the waitress his most open smile, the one he used to charm women all over Sydney.

"Do you think so? I'm pretty upset about how much the colour has faded." The waitress scrunched her face with worry.

"I don't just think so. I know so. And I bet she'll fit you in right after you finish your shift here."

"Okay. I believe you. Do you guys want menus, or something?"

Stu's smile stretched, and satisfaction made his torso warm. "Yeah, that'd be brilliant. Thanks." He strutted back to the table and sat on the wooden chair with his legs spread wide under the table, relaxed with all his focus on Poppy's gorgeous brown eyes. Little ribbons of black threaded through the brown of her eyes, adding depth to the colour.

Poppy shook her head. "You are something else. What did you do that for?" She pulled in a deep breath, and he had to force his gaze to stay on her face. Desperate for her attention, maybe…

After making him wait for far too long, she flicked her

hair over her shoulder. "How about we go out for a drink tonight, and maybe you'll get your kiss."

His breath rushed out of him. Thank fuck for a simple yes! Convincing the waitress in Poppy's favour had worked a charm.

The waitress slid two menus on the table. "How late are you open tonight?"

"At the salon?" Poppy asked.

"Yeah. I think you were right this morning. I want to get this shemozzle fixed."

"I'm so glad. It really bugs me to see a terrible job. Look, I'll discount the price for you too, since no-one should have to wear someone else's fuck up and then pay again to get it sorted out."

"Oh my god. He said you were a genius, but I reckon you are a life saver. Thank you so much." The waitress smiled. "I'll leave you to figure out what you want."

Stu waited until the waitress walked away. He reached out and laid his hands over Poppy's where they rested on the table.

"Thank you for the sales pitch."

"It's absolutely no problem. You sealed the deal with your offer of a discount. She'll be a client for life now." He smiled, confident, and gently rubbed his thumb over her wrist. Her pulse beat strong and fast, to match his. "Now, what do you want to eat?"

She scanned the menu. "The calamari with salad looks great."

"Excellent. I think I'll have the prawn linguine." He waved to his new friend, the waitress, who bounded over with some cold water. He ordered, then poured some water for Poppy.

"Do you want anything to drink? I'll have a flat white."

"A latte, thanks."

The waitress disappeared from Stu's vision, and he smiled at Poppy. A tiny part of him buzzed with a deep satisfaction. He'd waited too long before noticing Poppy. At first, she was merely a competent worker who solved a problem for him. And over time, he'd noticed more details about her. Quite similar to learning to play guitar; first the yearning to be able to play, and now the awkward, frustrating phase when it doesn't quite happen as quickly as you want. He couldn't wait until he played their song, perfectly in tune and in time.

"Do you like music?"

"Everyone likes music. Isn't a better question – what type of music do you like?" Poppy managed to take his simple query and reframe it.

"Yeah, okay. What music do you like?"

"Depends on my mood. Quiet reading music is different to angry cleaning music, or thumping dancing music." Her eyes glittered as she spoke, as if she knew he was imagining her dancing. Her body twisting and shaking to a wild tune.

He swallowed. "You clean your house while listening to thrash metal?"

"No. I need to be able to sing along with it. Old nineties grunge rock, like Frenzal Rhomb, or some of the classic Aussie rock ballads, you know, Acadaca, Cold Chisel." Poppy shrugged.

"Huh, I figured you'd be a new release banging pop kind of listener."

"You asked me about cleaning music. Old classics are great for cleaning for the same reason they are good for karaoke. Pop is better suited to an evening out. What about you?" She held up one finger in a wait gesture. "No, let me guess. You know the names of old paintings, I bet you listen to orchestral classical music."

"Why do you think that?"

"You seem like the type of guy who does everything to a plan." She paused, "and I bet you read once that listening to Mozart makes your brain better or some shit."

Laughter burst out and he rubbed his forehead. "That's quite the impression I've given you." He couldn't wipe the smile off his face at the way she met him on equal ground. Too many women wanted to fawn over him as a path to meeting his multi-millionaire business partner, Vince, or simpered and agreed with him because they thought he'd like it. He preferred honesty, although he'd played their game when he was younger while climbing up the ladder of success because it had been part of the lifestyle both he and they had chosen. Seeing Ella and Joey happy together had made him realise he'd been looking in all the wrong places if he wanted something more, and since he'd started looking, he'd noticed plenty of women who weren't like the social climbers he used to spend time with. His ego had led him astray, and he'd learnt over time to appreciate people who had the strength to steer him back to reality. Poppy's confident voice attracted him, for the simple reason that she wouldn't stand for any crap. He was saved from having to articulate any of these thoughts when the waitress came back with coffee.

"Your food is nearly ready."

"Thanks. Excuse me, what is your name?" Poppy asked the question he should have thought of asking ages ago.

"Josie."

"Thank you, Josie."

Josie nodded, and walked back to her post. She soon returned with their food, and the simple smells of fresh pasta, olive oil, and lightly cooked seafood filled the air. He nodded his thanks, once again, to Josie. Poppy sipped her latte, licking the foam away from her upper lip. His gaze followed her as she picked up her fork and stabbed her salad.

"Is everything alright?" Stu watched emotion flash across her face, before she half-smiled. She tapped her phone and glanced at the screen.

"Yes. Why?"

"You look a little uncomfortable, that's all."

"No, I'm fine. This salad looks amazing. How is your food?"

He glanced down at his linguini for the first time since it had arrived at the table. "It looks fine. Are you okay?"

"Yes. I'd better get back soon. Levi is holding the fort, and he gets a bit flaky if he doesn't eat properly."

"Why do I get the sense that you often miss lunch so that he can eat?"

"He's my apprentice. It's my responsibility to ensure his welfare."

"But who looks after you, Poppy?" Stu sensed a deeper

story behind the way she cared for Levi and he leaned towards her.

Her eyes popped open wide, then narrowed. "I do."

He kept his gaze on hers at the direct answer. "Then eat. Relax. Levi will be fine."

"You can't know that." She didn't meet his eyes, keeping her attention on her salad, as she started to eat, leaving him no option but to join her. The prawns were perfectly cooked, fresh, moist, and the linguini had an al dente texture, offset by the olive oil dressing. He ate quickly, barely registering the taste. If she worried about time, he'd give her a rapid lunch. Her yes had enough hesitation in it to maintain the possibility she might change her mind if he annoyed her. He glanced up from his food. She ate with the same careful efficiency she displayed at work.

"Are you enjoying that?"

"Yes. It's delicious. The dressing is perfect, with a touch of rosemary to go with the feta and olives."

He smiled. "I have a philosophy—"

"Do you now?" She smirked, her shoulders shaking a little, as she chewed.

"Yeah. I mean, it's not totally serious. God, you are determined to paint me as some kind of academic snob."

"You are the one who compared me to some random old painting, and who didn't disavow me when I mentioned Mozart. Now you have a philosophy?" She grinned over the top of her latte as she took another sip. And in one comment, she'd proven precisely why he craved her. She was the total package, fucking gorgeous, a hard worker, and hilariously sarcastic.

"My mother has a difficult relationship with food. I guess it stems from that, but I figure that if I'm going to eat it may as well be tasty."

"Oh, I'm sorry to hear that about your mum. As you've probably guessed from Spiro's… I'm Greek. Food is a huge part of our culture. It's more than food, it's about family, and time together."

"Does that mean that you judge the food based on the people who eat it with?"

"Pretty much."

"And—" He cocked his head and smirked with all his outward confidence, even though his heart skipped a beat. "How do I stack up?"

"Jesus, Stu, what type of question is that? You hardly need me to reassure you or boost your ego." Her eyes widened before she stabbed a piece of calamari with her fork.

"What does that mean?"

"Just take a look at us. You are the handsome executive, I'm just a fat hairdresser. The power balance is in your favour." Her self-depreciating comment made his veins pump with frustration.

"Poppy. You are not 'just' a fat hairdresser. You are beautiful, perfectly plump with a sunny smile, and competent fingers. You've got no idea what your curves do for me, have you?"

And that was without mentioning the way she put him in his place so succinctly. Her cheeks flushed pink, reflecting the heat in his own face. The sexual implication of her competent fingers made his skin ablaze for her. She stared at him, her fork hanging loose in her hand.

She shook her head slowly. "I have to get back to work."

"Shall I pick you up from the salon?"

"Straight from work? Are you kidding? Don't you know anything?" Poppy's feisty response made him grin.

"Oh right. You want to change and stuff?"

She chuckled. "I've got your number at the salon. I'll text you tonight and we can meet somewhere around eight."

"Cool." Relief rushed through his system. His attraction, built over such a long time, was worse than he'd thought. She inadvertently teased and tormented him until he was desperate enough to tell her the truth.

_____

4

"Poppy, I think you are fucking hot." Poppy couldn't get Stu's comment out of her head. Around and around it had gone all day, a ridiculous ear-worm as she tried to work. Luckily, the day had been full of the boring simple cuts that her grandfather's clients preferred. Or unluckily, perhaps. She could have done with a distraction. She'd raced home after lockup to get ready and now she stood outside her apartment, feeling overdressed in a floral print dress. It tucked in under her breasts and floated over the rest of her. She'd picked this dress because she loved the happy red, green, and white floral print. She'd paired the dress with her favourite red pumps, and a matching red purse. She might not be to everyone's taste, but she loved the way this dress floated around her body, filling her with confidence. Although…

She blew out a long breath, shaking her head a little. Stu's comment had floored her. She'd never imagined that someone like him, a tall, lean, advertising guy, obsessed with his image to the point where he'd deliberately get a silver fox look, would be interested in anyone who wasn't a bone-thin blonde model. And yet, his voice had been full of truth. The growl as he called her beautiful sounded like sex. Perfectly plump. She shrugged for the thousandth time that day. Maybe he just liked variety? Well, whatever. She intended to take advantage. No more would she wonder about his cock or the hard planes of his chest that she'd spied every time he came into the shop in summer, wearing just a cotton shirt and jeans hanging off his hips. After tonight, she would know. And she would keep the memory forever, no matter what happened. He'd asked who looks after her. She'd answered with the truth. "I do." And now she would look after her own pleasure too. With him.

She tapped her foot and glanced again at her phone. Her ride-share car was still two minutes away. Come on. Eventually the car arrived, and she confirmed the driver's id before she slid inside. Twenty minutes later, she slipped out the car, thanking the driver. She rated him five stars, as she walked focused on her phone, towards the bar. On the rare nights when she didn't have paperwork to do for the business, she came here with friends. The little suburban bar often had live jazz, and the moody lighting would be perfect for a first date. She'd once made the mistake of having a first date in a brightly lit restaurant, and the glare of the lights had made her feel like she was on stage, under a spotlight. Hardly conducive to relaxation and conversation. Why was she worrying about that now? She tucked her phone into her purse and ran her hands down her dress, smoothing out the fabric.

"Hey there. You came." Stu's voice came out of the shadows. He sounded surprised that she'd turned up, when she was the one stunned that he asked her.

"Here I am." She decided her only option was boldness, to grab what she wanted from tonight, so she stepped towards him, and pressed a kiss to his cheek. Her breasts brushed against his cotton shirt and she had to suppress a shiver of delight, as her nipples pebbled at the simple touch.

"Would you like a drink? I can grab something for you. What is your favourite? You know, this place is a great choice, really great." Stu's breath whispered on her cheek as he talked. Would it be too much to wrap herself against him? Her heart sped up, more than the usual thud whenever she cut his hair.

"The guy behind the bar with the spiky black faux hawk does a mean strawberry champagne cocktail, if you are man enough to order a girly drink like that."

"Poppy, you can't scare me off with an attempt to undermine my masculinity. I work in advertising. Nothing you could order will scare me." Stu leaned away from her, a wide grin spreading over his handsome features. The smile made his cheekbones seem even sharper, and his black hair, with her grey art at his temples, shone under the dull lights swaying from the ceiling. He waved at a stool as he turned towards the bar, so she slipped her purse over her head, the long red strap hanging between her breasts as she sat down, tucking her dress around her legs on the tall stool. Stu disappeared to the bar, his tall lean presence dominating the view, or perhaps that what just because she couldn't look away from him. His jeans hugged his tight arse. She grinned as she stared. SAAS, in action, on display for her. Stu really did have an incredible arse, she wanted to grab it with both hands and hold tight. Or better, grab those jeans, tug them down and expose his tight cheeks for her personal view. Talk about fantasies come true. Even after he'd said those words, 'you are fucking hot', she still pinched herself. He'd asked her out. He'd seen her at work, maybe he'd seen the real her, when she was lost in her craft as she created the fake silver fox look. Whatever it was that motivated him, Poppy determined that she'd take this chance and grab it with both hands. Literally.

"Here you go." Stu slipped the tall thin glass in front of her and stood so close beside her that she'd only need to lean sideways half an inch for her shoulders to brush against his chest. He placed a schooner beside her glass, the amber liquid at odds with her bubbles. A neatly cut strawberry rested in the bottom of the glass, and the barman had dipped the rim in soft sugar.

"Thank you." She twisted slightly on the chair, her fingers twitching on the stem of her glass.

"I love—"

"Tell me—" She spoke at the same time as Stu. Awkward. She giggled, hearing the nervousness in the sound.

"What do you love, Stu? Beer?" Poppy sipped her champagne, the sugar on the rim sweet on her lips quickly washed down by the dry sparkles of the bubbly fluid.

He blew out a short breath and it tickled the back of her neck. "Sure, I love a good beer as much as anyone, but I was going to say that I love your dress. It's so colourful, cheery. It really suits your hair."

She smiled into her glass, before raising her eyes to his. "You know me, hair comes first." How had she never noticed the ring of brown at the edge of his blue eyes? A glowing ring of fire.

"Hair comes first." He copied her, as if he wanted to keep notes about her stored away somewhere safe where he could access them later. A slow warmth started in her belly, like the coals on her father's precious BBQ when he blew on them in the morning to re-ignite them.

"But you can't work all the time. What do you do in the evenings, after work?"

"Umm, paint my nails and watch Netflix." She shook her head, unable to hide her sneer. "No, I do the account books, buy supplies online, pay bills, that kind of thing." What did he think she did? Did he assume she happily shaved old men's heads all day, then went home to her apartment and baked cakes for charity? If only she had time to bake for charity. She hid her sigh with another sip of her drink. Now wasn't the time to get all het up about her daily worries.

"Hold on. Are you saying you own Spiro's? I'd assumed you just work there." Stu spread his hands wide, the motion drawing attention to the way his shirt pulled tight across his chest. The fabric couldn't possibly hide the muscles underneath. He obviously had time to spend at a gym with the hints of rippled hardness under his shirt. Poppy's mouth watered, she ought to be upset at his assumption, but his body was so close that his citrus and thyme cologne over-whelmed her nostrils, and caught all her attention.

"Sorry, what did you say?"

"You own the hairdressing place? Spiro's?" Stu picked up his beer, drawing her gaze to his hands. He'd rolled up the sleeves of his cotton business shirt, and dark hairs covered his firm forearms. Would he have the same dusting on his chest?

"Yes." She took a short breath. Concentrate on talking. Stop staring at his body. "Yes, my Pappous, that's grandfa-ther in Greek, well, he started it in the late 1940s when they came here after the war. I helped him when his arthritis got too much and inherited the business when he died a couple of years ago. He'd be 91 next month if he was still around." She sniffed as the familiar grief floated around her. She hadn't meant to tell him that much. He rested his arm over her shoulders and rubbed his thumb at the base of her neck. His touch comforted her, with an undercurrent of the lust that shimmered whenever he was close. It should've been weird, the mix of two sensations, but she wanted to lean into him, to get more.

"Hey, I'm sorry I asked." Stu whispered in her ear.

She couldn't stop herself pulling away and frowning at him. "Why?"

"Because you are upset. I mean it's really cool that you run your own business. I didn't think. I just assumed, wrongly, that you worked for some guy called Spiro, even though I'd never seen him. But you know, maybe he was there on other days. Ella, she's the lawyer at work, would have my balls for assuming that you couldn't own the place, and now the story of your grandfather…"

"Stu. Stop talking." Did he know he talked too much when he was nervous? She leaned forward and pressed her lips to his. The sugar on her lips mixed with the tang of beer on his. It should have been wrong, but it was so right. He should have been hard, brutal, with that lean sinful body of his, but his lips were soft against hers. She'd only meant to reassure him with a swift peck, instead he welcomed her. The buzz of voices at the bar faded as she opened for him. He slid his hands into her hair, cradling her scalp.

"Poppy." His whisper floated over her lips.

"Just kiss me."

He nibbled her bottom lip instead, toying with her, sending little shards of pleasure rushing across her skin. She wanted him to follow those tingles with kisses down her throat.

"I can't, Poppy. I won't be able to stop." Holy shit. Really?

"Oh, come on. That can't be true."

He lifted his head. "You have no idea, do you? How much you push my control?" Heat bloomed on her cheeks, and a rush of joy flooded her lungs. She stared at him in disbelief.

"You need to stop saying things like that." She turned away and sipped her champagne, the bubbles chasing his taste away.

"Poppy—"

"Tell me more about your work. Your lawyer sounds—" She changed the subject, to give herself more time to process the apparent fact that Stu wanted her as much as she wanted him. Un-fucking-believable.

"My lawyer?" He shook his head, "Ella is Kapow's lawyer. I guess I just mentioned her because she's amazing. You'd really like her." His whole face lit up as he spoke, the truth of his words reflected in his expansive arm gestures. It would have been a joy to watch except for a niggling doubt. He hadn't lit up so much when saying the same thing about her.

"What's so great about her?" Her fingers toyed with the stem of her champagne.

"She's diligent and she's not afraid to tell anyone if they are wrong, even Vince."

"Vince?" she asked. She tamped down the jealously at Stu's excitement.

"He owns Kapow. Not many people stand up to him, he's a force to be reckoned with as a business leader, yet Ella is one of the few." He paused and peered at her. She sipped her champagne before she said something defeatist and out of character. She didn't come on a date with Stu to hear him carrying on about the female lawyer at work.

"I suppose she's gorgeous too." Poppy whispered into her glass. Working in advertising meant Stu was partly responsible for the way her body was seen on telly. She hated the way she only ever saw herself as a punchline or on weight loss programs with some bulked-up protein fuelled trainer screaming at miserable people who thought being skinny would make them happy. She'd love to see more representation of herself, plump and happy, on telly. The body shaming culture could get stuffed. She swallowed away the bitterness. This ugly internal tirade was based in one thing, and one thing only; she was jealous of someone she'd never met because Stu admired them. She plastered on a fake smile, pushing away her frustrations at the way the world saw her.

"Ella? I suppose so. I've never really thought about it, besides she's engaged."

Poppy felt a wave of relief wash over her, mixed with the guilt that came with irritational jealously. "What does that matter?" She tried to hide her emotions in a bland tone and probably didn't succeed if the cool expression on Stu's face was any indication.

"You sounded jealous of my colleague. It doesn't matter if she's engaged or not, but I thought it might clear that up for you. Although you might be jealous when you hear who she's engaged to." Stu grinned.

"Fine, I'll bite. Who?" Presumably someone famous.

Stu rewarded her with one of his charming grins. "He's a Dally M winner, a legend of the game."

"Which game?"

"Dally M winner." Stu stretched out the words as if they should mean something to her. She shrugged.

"League. Do you not watch—" Stu started.

"—Don't say it. Yes, I watch sport. Just not that one." She preferred proper football, soccer not league, or that weird footy they played in Victoria, and certainly didn't need Stu to articulate his assumption that her body shape prevented an interest in any physical activity. The rollicking swirl of desire and annoyance in her gut leapt to life again at the idea of getting physical with Stu. She couldn't trust his words about how he desired her. She yearned for them to be true, sure, but society's expectations added a bitter thread to every comment of his.

Years ago, she'd learnt not to trust a man's word. Her first job as an apprentice, with Jean-Phillipe, the most famous hairdresser in Sydney, had ended in disaster. Oh, not from a hair dressing point of view, she'd learned plenty of craft from his salon. The disaster came when he'd taken her enthusiastic naivety and stomped on it. After hearing his endless promises about her talent and career, she'd finally succumbed to his demands to be his lover. Her innocent belief in Jean-Phillipe's promise of mentorship for the world champs had been crushed when she'd found him in bed with someone else. She shook her head at the distasteful memory. Jean-Phillipe; a lesson in why she'd never trust an older charming handsome man again. She blinked at the memory. Stu wasn't older, he faked it, but it didn't help that he obviously loved his job with more passion than he had for his comments about her. He twisted towards her, his knees pressing against hers, as he held his hands, palm up, towards her.

"My apologies. I just assumed that everyone around here watches league. What do you like?"

She blinked. He wanted to know what she liked. Maybe all her doubt was just that, doubt. The light pressure of his knees against hers sent little spikes of pleasure up her thighs, and for a second she forgot the question.

"Stu, my family is Greek. There is only sport that we all adore." Soccer.

"What's that?"

"Roller derby." Poppy said the most ridiculous sport she could imagine, simply to see his reaction. He tilted his head and those lips of his twisted.

"Huh?"

"I'm jesting. Football, of course. The beautiful game. The only game, if you ask my father." She grinned as he shook his head at her.

"And here I was, imagining you in short pants, elbow pads and with the fierce make-up of roller derby skaters." Stu chuckled, his gaze dragging down her arms and body to rest at the point where their knees touched. She shoved him on the shoulder.

"Get out of here. No, you weren't."

He held up hands up in front of him, in that gesture that soccer players do when they appeal the ref's decision. "Come on now. Is it so hard to imagine that I desire you?"

She peered into his eyes, trying to determine the depth of truth. "It's a rather specific fantasy. Banging a roller derby enforcer." Contentment and longing settled over her as he barked out a laugh. Making him laugh again become her new goal, an absolute must to achieve more than once.

"What can I say? The idea is suddenly appealing." The intensity in his gaze made her glance away. She lifted her glass to her lips, tilting it so the strawberry in the bottom slid down into her mouth. His gaze focused on her exposed throat. The sweetness of the fruit took away the tart sharpness of the final drop of champagne. Why did his outrageous flirting make her so uncomfortable? Was it simply because she found it difficult to trust his intentions? She'd been here before; listening to a man's false compliments.

"Tell me something."

"Anything." Stu leaned forwards, closer, stealing her breath from her lungs.

"Who is this famous league player engaged to your darling colleague?" Poppy wished she could take away all the little hurts over the years that accumulated in that one snarky comment. It sounded out of place here, with him giving her his undivided attention. Damn her trust issues, and damn Jean-Phillipe to the hell he belonged in for making her doubt herself when she should be enjoying Stu's attention.

5

"Big Joey Mananui." Stu had to drag Joey's name from the depths of his brain as Poppy changed the subject away from taunting him. Imagining her in a roller derby uniform, with knee and elbow pads, tiny short pants, and ferocity in her glare, had him uncomfortably aroused for a public setting. He'd spent two years with her hands on his temples, watching her intense focus on her work, and feeling like the centre of the world as she listened to him pondering different work politics and scenarios. She relaxed him, made him feel comfortable as he explored his thoughts on various topics. He could scarcely believe she had finally agreed to take the next step with him, and she was even funnier outside of her work persona. And the casual way she referenced her family, as if they were an extension of herself, made him desire her even more. A bonus feature.

Growing up with just him and Mum hadn't seemed like he'd missed out on anything. His mum had worked extra hard to give him a found family—friends instead of cousins, father figures through sport and work. He hadn't been part of a big family, but Poppy's simple mention of hers made him wonder if he'd missed out by not having that. He shook his head. He appreciated Mum's efforts as a single mother, and the first thing he'd done with his first big bonus at Kapow, was buy her an apartment of her own. She'd struggled to pay the rent throughout his whole upbringing. She wouldn't struggle anymore. She'd given him the ability to earn big, and he would forever be thankful. Hence the flood of guilt churning in his gut whenever he felt the tug of a big family.

"Who?"

"Joey Mananui. He's a big name league player who had a spinal injury in a game a few years ago."

"Oh, him. Everyone in Australia has heard of him." Poppy smiled, a slow grin spread over her face. "You get to hang out with some pretty amazing people in that job of yours."

"Yes, a few." The tension in his shoulders and at the corners of his eyes eased. "One of the perks of the job, I guess."

"I guess?" A crease flashed between her eyebrows.

"Is that a problem?"

"No, it just illustrates the differences between us. I'm just a hairdresser, and you get to hang out with the rich and famous."

"Can you stop with the 'just a hairdresser' nonsense? There is no 'just' about it. You have mad skills."

"Mad skills? Are you sixteen?" She raised one perfectly

arched eyebrow. His teeth clenched for a long second as she deflected her ability once more, until she giggled.

"Thank you. It's not often someone recognises my talents."

"You should do more to advertise them."

"Probably." She paused, then grinned, her eyes glinting with humour. "I don't think we came here to talk about work; mine or yours."

"Tell me why we came here, then?" He held his breath, hoping she referred to his request for a kiss earlier in the day. Waiting for her answer made the pause drag on forever, even though it was only a breath or two.

"Mmm, I forgot." Her smile stretched, and he opened his mouth to answer when she winked. "I'm kidding. I've been hoping you'd ask for that kiss ever since you asked me out tonight."

The breath he'd been holding raced out in a rush. "I knew you couldn't resist me." He joked, rather than let her know how much this mattered to him.

"Stu. Shut up and kiss me… Again." Poppy put her empty glass down and placed her hands on his arms, just above his elbows. She leaned forward, only a fraction, but enough for her dress to gap slightly at the front, gifting him a glimpse of her heavenly breasts. He reached up and cradled her face in his hands, her soft skin against his palms filling him with warmth. She closed the gap, pressing her soft, lush lips against his. Everything inside him screamed possession. He had craved this kiss for so long, he wanted to crush her to him, to own her. Instead he taunted her, toying with them both, nibbling on her bottom lip, keeping his chest only lightly touching those bountiful breasts of hers. God, he had one fantasy, greater than all others. He wanted to fuck her breasts. To come on her neck, to spread his seed like a dirty necklace on her clean skin, as she fingered herself deep. His groan reverberated against her lips and she drank in the sound.

"Eww, take it home, you two." A heckler from the bar called out, invading their space. Poppy eased herself away from him, her breath rapid on his face as she paused an inch from him.

"Shall we?" He blinked as he realised he would have fucked her in public if no one stopped him. When had he ever been pushed so far that he'd forgotten his surroundings? And they'd only kissed.

"What? Go home?" Her voice sounded as though she'd just sucked his cock deep and bruised her throat. Hoarse, and oh, so, sexy. He grabbed her hand.

"Come with me." He tried to make it a command, not the desperate plea it felt from inside. She smiled, power and knowledge in her eyes, as she slipped off her seat and let him tug her out of the bar and into a cab. He sent a quiet thanks to Poppy for choosing to meet in a bar with a taxi rank at the front door.

Stu spent the entire cab ride, silent, thankful the dark evening light hid his desire for her. He was a fool for letting his fantasies run away during their kiss. In public. Like a foolish young man, not the confident executive he'd spent years fashioning himself into. What was it about her? He felt the driver's eyes on him and sensed Poppy glance at him on and off during the drive. His left foot pressed hard into the floor, as if he could speed up the driver. He wanted her in his house, where he could—finally—undress her, unwrap her and discover her. He'd already waited far too long for this. Two years. Two years of inconsequential little touches. He wanted the big strokes, to hold her properly. The cab pulled up outside his townhouse, and he tossed some cash, far more than required, at the driver.

"Thanks, mate." He swung his long legs out of the car, and paced around to help Poppy, only to find that she'd already exited the vehicle. She brushed her dress down, her hands tracing her voluptuous shape, a motion that only increased his longing for her.

"I would've opened the door for you."

"I don't need your old-fashioned chivalry." Poppy laughed, a loose relaxed sound. It filled his chest and raced over his skin.

"You're a modern girl, then?" He winked to compliment his joke, as he tried to brazen away the unsteady thrum in his abdomen.

"I'm not sure where to start with that. The girl comment, or the wink? Did you just wink at me?"

He couldn't work out if she was bemused or annoyed. "Did you like it?" He swallowed as he realised he'd spoken without thought. What a daft thing to say! She chuckled, and reached out for his hand, skimming her thumb over his wrist, using his own signature soothing move on him. Shards of sensation shot up his arm.

"Take me inside. … And stop talking, Stu."

He stared at her for a moment, then paced decisively up his front steps, holding her hand tight in his. Virtually dragging her inside. Caveman, like. This is what she did to him; she made him primitive. Well, she'd told him to take her inside…

He stood outside his front door, pulled his key from his pocket, then steadied his hand before he turned the key in the lock. The anticipation ratcheted up. She was here, finally, in his house. He pushed the door open and stepped inside.

"Welcome." He put the key back in his pocket, reached up and flicked on the light, and turned to shut the door. Only to find himself pushed back against the wall, Poppy's lips meeting his with the same frantic pace he needed. He wrestled for control, the passion between them threatening like an out of control bush fire, all heat and fury, sparks driven ahead on the wind. He threaded his fingers through her hair, that rainbow hair of hers, so bright and cheerful. She kissed with the same happiness, with the taste of sweet popping candy, refreshing and surprising. Sugary sweet with bursts of undeniable force. Or maybe it was the champagne and strawberry she'd had at the bar? His hands slid down her back, greedily touching her, until he grabbed her arse. So round and full in his palms. Glorious.

"Oh my god, Poppy. You'll be the death of me."

"I'd like a little death."

He broke the kiss "Did you say you want death?" A wave of confusion made him suck in a deep breath.

"It's an old fashioned term for an orgasm. Don't you read?" She grinned, and no wonder, as he felt his mouth drop open.

"I can help you with an orgasm, or a few… And yes, I read." He took one long step, pushing her up against the opposite wall in his hallway, one leg between hers. She sighed, almost a moan, and he bent to kiss her. Even though he towered over her, part of him registered her power in this situation. Her power over his control, as his desperation reached fever pitch for her. He deepened the kiss, probing her mouth. She responded, opening up, her tongue tangling with his, her hands spread on his back as he pressed her soft body up against the wall.

"Poppy." Two years of lust slammed him in the chest. She was all curves, all luscious woman, and he wanted to devour her. He kept his hands on the wall, the solid flat plane keeping him anchored to reality as she stroked his back. "There is a condom in my wallet."

Her hands slipped down, one tight on his arse, the other one on his wallet, tugging it free from his jeans. His hips rocked against her, his cock aching to be free from the fabric containing him. He took a half-step backwards, instantly missing her warmth, but necessary so he could plunder. Her eyes glinted, dark brown and heavy with desire, as she stared up at him.

"I've wanted you for so long." His voice croaked and her lips curled up in a sly grin, as if she knew she had all him tied in knots. Poppy lifted his wallet and flicked it open. She kept her gaze on his, as she slipped out the little foil packet and tucked it in his shirt pocket. Her fingers barely touched his chest muscle before she reached down again and replaced his wallet in his jeans. The whole motion was perfunctory, basic, erotic in its simplicity. Quick, but not fast enough. He was about to grab her dress, fling it upwards, when she did it for him. The fabric bunched around her waist, giving him a view of black lace and soft flesh. He grabbed his jeans to free his erection. He had to have her now. He'd waited too long already.

"Let me." Her voice was a whisper of breath against his stubble rough cheek. She wrapped her hands around his length and stroked. He hissed, closing his eyes. Oh, God.

"Stop."

"Why? Is it too much for you?" Her full lips, reddened from his kisses, stretched in a knowledgeable smile. He groaned and shook his head, wanting to beg for more, but he could only pant as her hands slid on his cock. She stroked him as if she worshipped him. His hips rocked into her hands, the point of explosion so near it took all his considerable strength to stop himself coming all over her. He pulled her hands off him, placed them on his butt, and let out a short steamy breath. To give himself a necessary moment, he plucked the condom out of his shirt pocket, ripped open the foil, and rolled it onto his cock. Ready.

"Poppy." His voice rasped, rough, as he cradled her head and kissed her deep. She bloomed under his ministrations, giving back with everything he asked for. All he could see and taste was Poppy. The Poppy he'd wanted for two long years. Why had it taken him so long to ask her out, to ask for this? He stroked her neck, down her throat, as he pressed her harder against the wall. Her breasts were the perfect soft pillow to his firmness, and he cradled the edges of them as he stroked his hands down her sides to those lacy underpants. She moaned into his mouth as he slid his fingers under the lace.

"Is it all rainbows down there too?" He nipped at her

bottom lip. She spread her legs for him, and his hand slipped between. Into perfect moistness. Her thighs trembled against him, as he pressed against her tight clit. She moaned into his mouth. He explored her wet pussy. She was as ready as him, and when he slid his finger deep inside her, she bit her bottom lip and her eyes widened.

"Please." She moaned and dug her fingers into his backside.

"First, come for me." He played with her, slick and beautiful, until she screamed, clenching around his fingers. He kissed her again, drinking in her sounds until she relaxed, slumped between him and the wall.

"Hook your leg around me." He shifted as she obeyed, his cock at her entrance, desperate for release.

"Now, please." She begged, clutching him with one leg, and both hands, dragging him inside. He thrust, hard and strong, slamming into her. Oh God, this was a heaven he'd become religious for. He fit perfectly, inside her tight, slick body. The religion of Poppy. He pumped into her, over and over, and she rocked with him, in perfect time, surrounding him until she screamed and came again and he followed. Hard. Furious. Everything he'd waited so long to achieve, resolved in a flash of light behind his eyelids, his heart thundering in his chest.

"Poppy. You are wilder than my imagination, and that takes some doing." He grinned as he slid out of her and wrapped his arms around her waist. "Come to bed with me."

She gasped. "Oh my word, we've hardly made it inside the house." She glanced around him, and chuckled.

"I told you I was keen for you."

"Keen? Any keener and we'd be fucking on the front door step with the world watching."

"Maybe one day." Stu grinned as she shook her head.

"Nope. I'll fuck you anywhere in private, but there is no way you'd get me so unabandoned that I'd do you, or anyone, in public."

His smile disappeared at her mention of other people, a stark reminder of the difference in their desire. He might have lusted after her, enjoyed her banter, for two years, but this was all new to her. A one-off lark, perhaps.

"I'd like to think I can fulfil you enough that you won't need to think of anyone else. After tonight, you'll be branded with my taste, and you won't stray."

She smacked him in the shoulder. "Well, someone has a big—" Her gaze dropped to his softening penis, still latex covered, and his open jeans, then back to his eyes. "Ego."

6

———————

Poppy stood on jelly-like knees in his hug, her back pressed hard against the wall, and her underwear still mostly in place, in the aftermath of delicious, frantic sex in Stu's hallway. He babbled on about something. Did this man ever stop talking? Oh, his words delighted her. He spoke as if she was the centre of his world, and she wanted to believe him. But he worked in advertising. He probably couldn't switch off the overly positive commentary. Yet the remark about how he'd brand her with his taste made her want to fan her cheeks. *Yes, please.*

"Come with me. I'll show you big." Stu stepped backwards. Her dress fell, fluttering down, as he tugged her hands. His firm hands wrapped around her wrists, as he walked backwards down his hallway, his focus still firmly on her. Was this desire or protection she felt? And how did he make her feel safe and wanted as he man-handled her? He was possessive. Cave-man-esque in modern clothes. The angel on one shoulder told her she should hate being dragged around metaphorically by her hair, while the devil sung about the glories of Stu's expectant, virtually dauntless attitude towards her submittal to him.

"Oh, this is gorgeous."

"It's okay for Surry Hills. It's a nice space for entertaining." He dropped the used condom into a bin in the kitchen.

"It must be lovely in the evenings." Her eyes must be bugging out on stalks as she took in all the little details. His place was beautiful, modern and clean with new appliances. Nothing like the shabby old unit she rented. She could live above her shop, but it made financial sense to rent out that space, and rent a smaller, cheaper unit for herself, further from the city.

"You can leave your purse here if you want." His gaze raked over her dress, settling between her breasts. She glanced down, the red strap on her purse hung between her boobs, and the fabric was all ruffled after their wild, entrance-way sex. Her face flamed with arousal as she slid the purse over her head, and Stu's gaze followed her hands. Simply taking off her purse under his perusal had her turned on and ready again. Holy fuck, she wanted him to undress her because the promise of glory in his eyes made her glow all the way through. Scratch that, she wanted to undress for him, to reveal herself with absolute control over the sparks between them.

"Come upstairs with me." He turned towards a set of stairs, and reached out to hold her hand, and started to climb. She followed, one step behind him, so close that she could almost kiss his lower back. His jeans hugged his hips as he walked, giving her the perfect view of his gorgeous arse. They reached the top, every step emphasising his lean strength. Her heart raced, not from the stairs, from his proximity, from the idea that he wanted her again. He'd pretty much dragged her into his bedroom, giving her no doubt about his lust. She could meet his lust on even footing. She wanted to strip that shirt from him, to see his firm body. She'd felt him pressed hard against her, every muscle burnt against her softer flesh as he'd pounded into her downstairs. This time she wanted to watch. She wanted the visuals of his body imprinted in her memory. She wanted to taste him, and not just his kiss.

"Are you okay?" He gave her hand one more tug, pulling her towards him.

"I'm just great, thanks." She spoke the truth, with a little smirk to protect herself against the sexual tension in the air. He leaned towards her and kissed. Nothing like the indecent kiss in the hall, this one was sweet, soft, welcoming. His masculine scent had a citrus note, with herbal undertones, a sophisticated, mellow smell that reminded her summer fruits eaten on a picnic blanket under a fig tree. Surprisingly tangy. Her mouth watered at the thought of licking his flesh, tasting the rest of him. He immediately deepened their kiss, as if he could read her thoughts. What kind of magician was he? Before she could expand on that thought, sensation overwhelmed as Stu sucked on her tongue. Her knees weakened. His hands spread on her back, supporting her. Her eyes fluttered. Stu gentled his kiss again, nibbling at her bottom lip. Shards of pleasure pulsed down her throat drawn out by Stu's clever ebb and flow of intensity. She reached up and placed her hands on his shoulders, hesitant to run her fingers through his hair. Would that be too much like work?

"You can touch my hair if you want. It won't be weird, I promise." Stu kissed her lips with a perfunctory peck.

"I think it would be pretty weird." She glanced around the room.

"But you love hair, and I enjoy your touch. God, Poppy, why do you think we are here?"

She shrugged, her breasts shifting against his hard chest as he held her tight. "Um, is that a trick question?"

"No." He smiled, his eyes dancing. "I asked you out, hoping for this, because your touch in my hair is amazing. And I couldn't stop wondering about you touching the rest of me."

"Oh." Poppy felt like the floor had disappeared from under her feet. He'd wondered about her touch. She blinked and tilted her head to the side.

"Are you okay?"

"Yes. I'm just contemplating where I should start."

"My cock." Stu's voice rumbled with confidence, and his grin matched the sparkle in his eyes.

"Don't get too greedy." She didn't hide her smile. "We have plenty of time."

"Best start with my hair then." He bowed his head for her, an irreverent gesture that she deliberately ignored. He wanted her to touch his hair, well, she wanted to touch his firm chest and odds were that he'd have a sprinkling, or more, of hair there for her to thread her fingers through. She let her hands drift down to his shirt, tracing the open collar. His breath sped up against her neck as she explored the small triangle of skin before flicking open one button, then another, until his shirt hung loose and her hands rested at his waist band. His black hair against surprisingly tanned skin drew her eyes up his abdomen in a line to his broad chest. Did he work out without a shirt? Her lips parted, and her breath sped up.

"Touch me." Stu commanded; his tone made her wonder why she paused. She spread her palms over his stomach, the wash-board abs tensing under her touch, sending a sizzle through her fingertips and up her arms. She shivered.

"Are you cold?" He stroked her bare arms, his warm hands over her skin was delightful as he calmed her gooseflesh. Caused by him and soothed by him.

"Not cold." Poppy whispered, throaty and needy. She explored his chest with her fingers, the strength in his pecs with the perfect amount of chest hair over them. Masculine. She never understood the current fashion for hairless men, perhaps because hair was her thing. She loved the feel of it under her fingers, the way it slipped through over her hands, how she could smooth it, or frizz it, or shape it. She traced his muscles, played with the small black hairs, brushing them this way and that, until he grazed his hands up her neck and held her cheeks.

"Poppy."

"Yes?" She looked up at him to see a puzzled expression

on his face, as if he wanted to understand her. His black eyebrows framed his blue eyes. Rough black stubble had started to emerge on his cheeks. All that black hair, with only her crafted silver highlights on his temples.

"When I said touch me, I didn't mean for you to create patterns on my chest. I meant…"

"I know what you meant, Stu. What is the rush?"

"No rush." He bent his head and kissed her forehead, gentle and tender. Suddenly, she didn't want tender anymore. She grabbed his head and dragged him down for a kiss. A full, open mouthed, tongue battling kiss that made her knees weak and her core bloom with heat. A kiss that made her wetter, ready for him again. He responded with controlled energy, and every stroke of his tongue was designed to make her moan. She pushed his shirt off his shoulders, her hands scrambling to keep pace with his kiss.

"Can I take your dress off?" He punctuated his question with little kisses over her cheek towards her ear.

"Yes." A shiver of sweetness spread over her skin. How incredible to ask her, given that they'd already fucked like wild bunnies in the hallway. His question implied she could walk away at any point, safely, if she wanted. It made her want to stay even more, sending a fresh zing of desire humming through her body. His hands roamed over her back, and she melted into them.

"Where is the zip?"

"Down my left side."

He kissed her shoulder and bent to look at her side. "That's surprising. You are a bundle of surprises, my Poppy."

She should rail against his possession but for once she

believed him. She still couldn't believe he'd asked her out—he was someone important and she was just her—but their frantic fucking in the hallway just now couldn't be invented. It surprised her, but he really did want her as much as she wanted him. His fingers didn't hesitate as he unzipped her. His hand slid inside her dress, cupping her breast. She sighed, almost a moan as he brushed his thumb over her nipple. The way he teased her and taunted her, closer to pleasure, then with small breathing spaces whenever he talked. She could listen to his rich masculine voice all day. And now his breath whispered in zephyrs on her neck as he explored.

"Fuck, I love your boobs." He fondled her, caressed her until her back arched and she moaned, wanting more. Her body, warmed up from their earlier efforts, now begged him for pleasure. She slipped her arms out of her dress, let it gape for him. He tugged it down and she loved the way his eyes widened as he unveiled her body. Her favourite black lace bra with purple ribbon bow had seemed hopeful when she put it on. Now, to see his gaze on her, she felt like a queen, a goddess.

"My God, Poppy." He breathed, his breath warm on her skin as he buried his head between her breasts, leaving her standing with her chin grazing his hair. Rational thought fled, even the sight of his bed, couldn't make her move as he worshiped her. Her legs softened as he played, his stubble on her breasts rough on her skin, then soothed by his mouth as he licked along the edge of her bra. Her hands hung over his shoulders, able only to grip him loosely for balance. He tugged her bra down to expose her pebbled nipples. He tweaked one and she let out an almost scream as pleasure coursed through her, down to her wet core. Her knees turned to jelly, and she sagged against him. He caught her, one hand on her lower back, and helped her walk the few steps to his bed.

"Sit down." His words barely filtered through as she let him guide her. Her dress hung askew around her waist, messy to go with the riot of sensation in her veins. She wouldn't normally be so passive, but no one had ever put her first in this game. Oh, many had lusted after her boobs, they were full and quite spectacular, if she did say so herself. Too many men stared rudely at her which gave her unwanted chills. Only Stu made her feel wanted, heated, with his commanding skill and his devoted regard. She wanted to rip off her bra, fling it across the room, and beg him to bury his face in her breasts. She leaned back on his bed, arms behind her for support as she watched him undress. Oh golly. Her imagination had nothing on reality. His body flexed and rippled as he slid his shirt off one arm, then the other. She licked her lips, swallowing, as he bent over and undid his shoes. She crossed her legs, and leaned forwards to get a closer view. His feet were huge, encased in neat black socks. She couldn't move, captured in place by the sight of him. Lean, strong, the very essence of a man. And he wanted her. The very thought almost brought her to an orgasm.

"Come here." Poppy managed to speak as he straightened, completely nude. His erection jutted out, thick and ready, in a bed of black curls. She reached out for him, curling her fingers around his length. His sharply inhaled breath made her own lungs work faster. She steadied herself, her fingers gliding on his slick skin.

"Poppy!" He reached down to drag her fingers away. She leaned forward, pushing away his hand with her other hand, all the while stroking his length.

"I'm supposed to be pleasuring you." Stu sounded like he spoke through gritted teeth.

"This is a pleasure for me." She shook her head, her rainbow shoulder-length hair floating around the edges of her vision. His breath was ragged, in time with her strokes. Poppy licked her lips. She bent down to kiss the end of his cock, sipping at the pre-come beading on the top.

"Fuck, Poppy. You shouldn't do that."

"Why?" Curiosity infused her voice. Did he have an aversion to being sucked off?

"What if I have a disease? I don't, but you should have asked. You need to be careful and look after yourself." Stu had a desperate raspy edge to his voice, the sound of barely held control. She wet her lips with her tongue and took him into her mouth. Only a fraction. Enough for Stu to growl, his fingers tightening on her shoulders. She pulled back until the end of his cock rested against her lips.

"It's kind of too late for that discussion, isn't it?" She gave him a little flick with her tongue.

"Well—" Stu gently pushed her shoulders back, easing her away from her prize, and looked deep into her eyes. "Not really, I mean, we used a condom before, so that should be fine. But you can't put come in your mouth without checking."

"Don't you think that should be my risk to take? And I

hope you aren't assuming that you didn't need to ask me, because I'm bound to be clean?"

"What? No, I mean, sure, let's have the conversation."

"We are. I'm clean. Are you?"

"Yes." Stu's gaze stayed intensely on hers.

"Ok. I guess that's sorted that. Unless either of us is lying." She shrugged. The conversation mattered. Just his timing sucked. Ironically. She started to bend down to continue, only to be halted by his firm hands.

"I want to kiss you all over."

"Maybe I want that too." She meant to kiss him everywhere, but found herself pressed back into the bed, with the weight of his naked body on her semi-clothed one. Heavy. Necessary. He covered her mouth with his, kissing her deep, taking away her breath and her ability to argue with him. Funny how much she'd started to enjoy arguing with him. He liked to command her, often making her bristle, although she'd already realised he didn't expect her compliance. Other times, he'd say the sweetest comment, like just now, to make sure she was safe. If his plan was to make her squirm with desire for him, to open herself up to enjoy being with him, then it worked an absolute treat. She drank in his kiss, the fragrant notes of his cologne, the remnants of his beer on his tongue, and the taste that was wholly Stu. Hers to taste and devour. He ran his fingers through her hair, spreading it on the bed around her head. She couldn't see, but she could imagine, a rainbow halo surrounding her. She wrapped her arms around him, her fingers investigating his long back muscles. The grove of his spine with strong muscles on either side, and each rib, moving in and out as he breathed. Rapid to match her own thundering pulse. His kiss went on and on, his tongue stroking hers, demanding her response. She slid her hands down, reaching as low as she could, around that gorgeous arse of his. The only she'd dreamed about many, many times. Now hers. In her hands. And he was firm, strong, perfect. Her own Stu's Arse Appreciation Society moment. Just for her.

7

_____

Stu kissed her as she explored his back with her fingers. He wanted this to be brilliant for her, better than a quickie in the hallway. A mind blowing quickie to be fair; for him anyway. He hoped she had been as thrilled as he had. She was his Poppy, the one he'd waited so long to have in his bed. He could sustain any amount of arousing torture this time around, all in the aim of keeping her here. It made sense from a strategic point of view; take your time, make her moan, make her cry with pleasure, and she'll want more. Again and again. There was no point in waiting two years for a quick fuck, although the frantic rush in the hallway had been more than his vivid imagination could have painted. Poppy was everything he desired in a woman. Quirky, creative, strong-willed, competent, and of course, plump and curvy in all the best ways. He ought to have been born in the Rubenesque era when women were glorified for their curves. He wanted to stretch this out and make it last.

She grabbed his arse, her fingers pressing into the

muscle, pulling his hard cock against her soft curves. Fuck, she was everything he'd dreamed of. Perfectly womanly, and oh, so responsive. He nibbled her bottom lip, then kissed a line down her throat. Her eyelids flickered shut, and when he cupped her breast, a little whimper emerged from her lips. He took his time, worshipping her beauty, sucking her nipples and loving the sounds of her enjoyment. His never-ending commentary flowed through his head, and he used the stream of words to inspire his mouth on her body, until the words just chanted Poppy, Poppy, Poppy. Her hands slipped up his back, resting between his shoulder blades as he tasted his way down her body. He pushed the rest of her dress down, little splashes of red flowers in his vision, against her soft skin. He kissed the creases left by her clothes, the little lines marring her skin caused by the seams in her dress. Every curve, every dimple, every indent, he traced with fingers and tongue, making notes of what made her moan as he made his way down her body to her ultimate prize. He could listen to her throaty noises of pleasure all night.

"Poppy…"

She lifted her head. "Mmm, yeah?"

"Can I undress you?"

"God, yes. Rip it off. Touch me."

The corner of his mouth quirked upwards. "Where?" He couldn't resist teasing her.

"You know where."

"Ask nicely."

She growled, like an infuriated kitten. "There should be a name for men like you. Pussy tease. Goddamn, just fuck me already."

He grinned, shifting further, until he settled between her legs. Could she get any more amazing? He lifted her hips and pulled her dress down, revealing black and purple lace. A skimpy scrap of fabric that barely covered anything. His head spun as all his blood rushed south. Fuck, if he wasn't hard before, he was ramrod stiff now. Poppy's fingers trailed over his head, reminiscent of every hair appointment, but different because her musky feminine scent filled his nostrils. He paused, to slow his stupidly fast breathing, letting each long breath out over her pussy. Her fingers clenched on his temple.

"Maybe I am a pussy tease. I can wait here all night." He lied, purely to prolong the anticipation building in her body. Her fingers strengthened against his scalp.

"I can't. Stu—" She cried out.

"You haven't asked yet." He tortured himself for her.

"Stu, please." She writhed under his hands, still resting on her lush hips.

"Please what?"

"Fucking hell. Anything, Stu. I need you." Every word uttered on a breathy tone, as she begged him to fulfil his promise. He traced his finger inside her lacy panties, and her thighs trembled with anticipation.

"You want me to touch you here?"

"I want you to fucking kiss me there. I want your tongue inside me. I want your cock inside me. Fuck, Stu. Stop pissing around and get on with it."

He chuckled against her stomach. That's what he wanted. For her to be as desperate as him. He wrenched her panties off, revealing all her glorious beauty. Only a thin landing strip of curls with the rest bare.

"Every hair is perfect. I should have guessed." He chuckled against her thigh, letting the sound reverberate against her skin. She trembled.

"Stu." She dragged his name out on a long syllable, making his smile stretch. He traced circles on her legs, teasing her with his touch.

"Let me guess, you want me to stop…" He deliberately paused.

"Don't. … Stop." She managed to pant out the helpless command, and it was everything he waited for. He shifted, requiring only a subtle change, so his mouth covered her completely. He darted his tongue out, tasting her feminine musk, flicking at her clit so the bundle of nerves made her beg and moan. She made the best noises as she bucked under his ministrations, as he slaked his thirst for her. When he fucked her with his tongue, she clutched the bed and screamed his name. His body filled with hot pride as he drank in her orgasm, her body shaking and clenching around him. It would be so easy to fuck her now, as she lay senseless on his bed, and he coveted pounding into her with every fibre of his body.

"Fuck me hard now." Her words slurred slightly, drunk on the pleasure he'd given her, and his body roared into action. He leapt to his feet, grabbed a condom from his bedside table, rolled it on and sank deep into heaven. She sighed, a long deep groan, as he filled her, and his heart hammered in his chest. Poppy curled her feet around his back, pulling him towards her, her heels pressed into his buttocks.

"Like this?" He managed to ask; his voice rough.

"Faster. Harder." She grabbed his arms, tugging him against her, as he drove himself into her. Over and over. Her hips bucked to meet him, until they pounded together, unable to form words, only desperate sounds. Slick. Fast. Hard. Into oblivion. Her orgasm made him come in a flood, finally losing control as he slammed into her. His Poppy. He slumped on her, nuzzling into her neck as his body gave a final few jerks at the end of his release. Her hands floated up his back, and into his hair, cradling her head against her. His last thought before he fell into a dreamy snooze was to roll them both sideways, so he didn't crush her. The clamber of words in his head had finally gone silent.

He dealt with the condom, then slipped back beside her with heavy eyes. Eventually he stirred; fuck knows how much later.

Poppy wriggled against him. "Sorry, I didn't want to wake you."

"Don't go." He tightened his arm around her.

"I'm not going anywhere. I was only untangling my clothes."

"Excellent. Get nude." His eyes flicked open and tried to see the glorious woman in his arms. Night had arrived while they'd rested. He could barely see his own hand resting on her waist. He half-rolled away from her and flicked on the lamp beside his bed. Shadows painted her and his gaze roamed over her bare skin.

She wrinkled her nose at him as she grinned. "You have a one track mind."

"I am a bloke. It comes with the territory."

"I suppose a joke about claiming me as your territory will be the next thing you say?" Her smile remained, her eyebrows raising a fraction.

"Now, you see, that's not true. You are an independent woman who owns a business. No one is going to claim you without your say." He saw hunger flash in her eyes and he knew she aspired to such control over her life.

Poppy rolled her eyes, her upper lip slightly curled upwards. "Nah, you over-estimate how much I control my own life."

"Truly?" He was lost for words.

"Yeah, I'm rolling in the cash, doing high end fashion hair for Sydney's elite, while enjoying lunches on my boat during the weekends." Funny how her sarcasm only highlighted how much she desired the life she described.

He scratched his temple. "All businesses have to start somewhere. You have the ability, you have the space in central Sydney, almost all the elements for success are in your reach."

"Except?"

"Except, you are afraid to take a risk."

She thumped him, hard, on the chest, and scrambled to sit up. "Fuck you, Stu. You don't get to make judgements on my life without all the facts."

"What?" He sat up and stretched his hands out before him. "I'm only trying to help. Market strategy is what I'm good at. Great at."

"Maybe I don't want, or need, your help. Maybe I'm just here for the sex." She flung her underwear off her ankles, where he'd shoved it earlier, and stood up.

"Hey, come here to me."

"Give me a second, will you?" She marched into his ensuite. He'd just had the best sex of his life, twice. And it took some doing to knock a few of his adventures off the list. Poppy made everything in his past pale and faint, like those times with others only mattered so he'd be practiced enough for tonight. Good for her. Maybe it was simply because he'd waited so long. The anticipation. He leapt to his feet, pacing back and forth. Perhaps that's why she could doze, then wake up and argue with him, because this was all new to her. The toilet flushed, and he spun towards the door. She stood in the doorway, completely nude, mostly in shadow.

Poppy froze as Stu stormed towards her. He cradled her face, kissing her full and firm before she could protest. Anger hummed in her veins at the way he wanted to advise her about her business. She knew it wasn't the dream she hoped for, but it was hers. She didn't need some bloke to state his opinions on what she ought to do, especially when he didn't have all the facts or understand the obligations she had to meet. She met his gaze and his kiss with all the energy flowing in her and took everything he could give her. Their tongues and teeth clashed, his stubble rubbed her soft skin, and she wanted the gravel rash she would have tomorrow. Wanted his marks on her as proof she was strong enough to take it. She wrapped her arms around his muscled waist and stepped against him. Skin on skin seared her already hot body. Pushing against him, she marched him backwards towards the bed. He jerked to a halt when his knees hit the bed, and she shoved him on the chest. He didn't budge.

"Oh, come on." She stopped kissing him to protest. "At least sit down when I ask."

"You didn't ask. You demanded." His blue eyes glittered, with amusement or warning?

Poppy half-grinned. "You wanted me to be strong and to take charge of my life. I'm in charge here. Now."

"Yes, boss." He spoke sardonically, and met her gaze straight on, with his hard cock wedged against her stomach. His enjoyment of her command apparent in the way she could feel it press against her.

"Sit down. Legs apart. You can only touch me from the waist down." She sank down with him as he sat, until she knelt between his knees. He couldn't reach anything below her waist, leaving him no option but to lean backwards on the bed. Just as she planned, and almost exactly like her many fantasies of him, stretched out nude for her. His large cock full and erect in front of her. She gazed up at his, hunger making her salivate. She had made him king of his domain, with her as his queen kneeling before him. The heady combination of power and lust as she raked his body with her eyes made her shiver. She hadn't touched him yet, and the waiting fuelled the fire in her belly. In his too if the tension in his muscles meant anything. His washboard stomach, with gorgeous hard muscles, quivered as she blew gently onto his cock. The thick shaft lifted towards her as he shifted his hips and pressed his knees against her shoulders. His touch seared her, sending a wave of arousal into her already wet core. The simple act of kneeling before him in worship had her wet and ready, especially knowing that he would impale her again as soon as she gave the command.

"I said you couldn't touch me above my waist." She didn't raise her voice, issuing the order in a breathy whisper. He forced his knees apart, only millimetres from her skin. She licked her bottom lip. His hips strained towards her, an act of begging for her touch. A move of desperation that she felt deep in her veins as heat surged inside her, and her breath panted shallow and needy. With one finger, she lazily traced a small circle on the broad head of his cock, then traced a line down the side over the long veins. His hands clutched handfuls of the bed cover, his knuckles white, and his thighs tense. His stomach muscles rippled.

"I have to touch you." The gravel in his voice sounded like begging, and she loved that she could make him sound so desperate.

"If you touch me, I'll stop." She taunted him, as a fresh wave of heat flowed into her core at the dark need written in his eyes. Her fingers explored, slowly, lightly, teasing him as he'd teased her earlier tonight, until the moment she cupped his balls, and he growled from the back of his throat.

"Patience." Poppy's whisper disappeared as she bent her head and licked his cock.

He hissed between clenched teeth. "Put your mouth on me."

She shook her head, letting her long colourful hair sway around her shoulders, the ends touching his thighs. The twitch of muscle as her hair stroked his skin made her smile. The satisfaction of having him displayed and at her mercy made her relish the power. She wrapped her hair around her hand to form a brush, and flicked it over his stomach, the ends whipping his skin with a soft lash. Strong enough not to tickle, light enough not to hurt him as the strands grazed his belly.

"Poppy." He breathed out her name on a plea, so she brushed him again. His abdomen tightened, each muscle bulging with tension. She stretched out her arms, lifting them to rest on his thighs, an action which made her breasts rub against the inside of his thighs. She lifted her gaze to his face to see his hooded eyes stare with longing at her. Sparkles of arousal tingled across her skin, as she brushed her hair over his cock.

"Oh, God, Poppy. That's amazing." His hips lifted again as she slid her hair up and down his length. Her breath blew in time with his vocal responses as he pumped his cock into her hair. As much as she loved taunting him, she wanted him to last long enough to fuck her, so she stopped.

"Don't stop." His command made her mouth dry, and she licked her lips. She wound her hair around his penis, sliding the loop up and down. Not a hand job, a hair job. A total experiment on her part.

"Holy hell." His expletive filled her with a heady warmth. Her idea worked, so she continued up and down until his shaft, all wrapped up like a present in her hair, became the centre of the universe.

"Poppy. I have to touch you." His voice was as rough as the surge of pleasure it gave her. He sounded like a glutton, needing more. More of her. Her silken wet core clenched at the thought.

"Not yet." She shifted, her hair sliding off his skin, as she took him into her mouth. Her lips gliding on his cock, from tip to as much as she could take, until he filled her throat. Back and forth, building pressure. His head fell backwards as she flattened her tongue and sucked him, worshipped him with her lips and mouth.

"That's enough." He pulled her hair, not enough to hurt her, just enough to release him from the glories of her mouth. She lifted her face towards his, feeling slightly dazed as he pulled her to her feet. Completely nude before him, except for her hands covering her stomach. She didn't have a fashionable thin stomach, and even plump girls in literature had slim waists. Not something she could claim.

"Don't hide from me. I want to see all your curves." It was greedy of him to demand this of her and she tried not to flinch.

"I need to see you before I bury myself in you." Oh, wow. She dropped her arms to her sides, utterly convinced by the decadent desire in his voice.

"Are you alright?" He held his breath.

"Yes." She didn't hesitate. She was his queen, who he desired in her entirety. He wrapped his arms around her hips and slid his hands over her belly.

"Your soft, round curves are everything. And all mine. Poppy." She kissed him hard, to demonstrate how much his words mattered. How desperately she loved being told she was sexy. Their kiss tasted like his cock, a little salty from the pre-come on her tongue and she loved it. His hands cupped her breasts as he commanded her with his tongue. Probing deep, in the rhythm he wanted to fuck her, rough, flesh against flesh. Pleasure gifted and stolen from each other in a tug of war that could only end with both of them wrung out. He pinched her nipples and she sagged against him, crying out with pleasures. He slid one hand around her back, supporting her as her knees weakened under his assault. He turned them both to lay her on his bed, covering her body with his, their skin slick with sweat and heat.

"I want to fuck you so hard." He shifted and pulled one nipple into his mouth. This time she screamed out loud, her breasts heaving, and her fingernails scratching his back.

"Do it." She wrapped her legs around his arse, opening for him.

"Holy shit, Poppy. Condom." He stretched out to the drawer and grabbed a foil. She snatched it from him, ripped open the packet, and rolled it on. The whole frantic motion robbed her of breath as his muscles moved athletically in the act of safety.

"Now." She pressed her heels into his arse, commanding him with her body and her voice.

"Ask nicely."

"No. Fuck me now. Hard. That's what we both want."

He pressed his cock into her entrance. "Like this?" Teasing her until she squirmed.

"More." Her feet dug into his backside, pulling him deeper inside her. She wanted to be filled by him, to have the beautiful length inside her, hard and fast. He plundered, just as she wanted, and she shivered letting out a long moan. He kissed her with the same ferocity she needed, taking her moans into his mouth. She sucked his tongue, words beyond her now, and he slammed his cock deep inside her on a single thrust.

"Yes. More. Stu." Her words flew out of her, uncontrolled, as he thrust into her again and again. Her hips lifted to join his, their skin slippery as she clenched around him. He grabbed her hips, deepened the angle, pleasure surging over her nerves. Her release broke in a torrent, ripping through her as he pounded into her deep. He pulled out, flipped her over, and slammed back inside from behind. The new angle drew out more pleasure until their cries joined, a drastic music of animal passion. And when he reached under her to graze his fingers over her clit, she shuddered and shook, the waves of fulfilment spiralling to a new place of sexual intensity. He buried himself deep as they came together.

8

———————

Stu lay back on the bed, his body happily exhausted, the warm dark Sydney night surrounding them both.

"You and your hair are such a talent." His vivid imagination had never conceived such an idea. Slippery like a blowjob, but tighter thanks to the strength in her hand. A mind-blowing collection of sensation. He'd almost come then, had to give himself a breather, and even then, he'd almost forgotten to get a condom in their mutual quest for pleasure.

She winked. "You mean, I'm good with hair."

"Yes. You are brilliant with hair." The double entendre seeped in, and an idea sprang up. He'd assumed she was afraid to take a risk with the business, but what if she just didn't understand marketing? He could help her achieve her dreams.

"Have you thought about upgrading the signage on your business? Spiro's doesn't exactly tell the world about the genius of Poppy inside."

"Yes, I've thought about it. It's not that simple."

"Why?" He turned to stare at her, lying in the shadows of his bedside table lamp. She should have been relaxed, sated but her eyebrows were drawn together. He reached up and rubbed at the indent. "The world should be told about your skill."

"Are we still talking in euphemisms here, or about my business?" She chuckled quietly.

He half sat up on his elbow. "I'm not sharing you with anyone, not in this sphere. Not after tonight." Her eyes widened and gratification filled his torso with warmth. "I refer, of course, to your business, I want you, and Spiro's, to be a great success. You deserve it."

"Because you've had a good root? That doesn't give you the right to put your nose in my business." Her voice was sharp.

"Hold on. I want to help you. Give me some credit. I've wanted to help before tonight. You are a genius with hair. No one has ever noticed that mine is fake, and it's been a massive assistance in my career."

"Okay." She drew out the word on a long cautious note.

"I mean, we'd be a great partnership. I'm a marketing superstar."

"Are you now?" She grinned and raised one eyebrow.

"Yes."

"And not short of ego too."

"It's not all ego. Some, maybe. Mostly it's just reality. I wouldn't be where I am unless I had plenty of talent."

"And you want to use that to improve Spiro's?" Poppy still sounded cynical and he wasn't sure why. He hadn't been faking when he spoke about his skills, so she should trust him with this. Persuading customers was his true talent in life.

"Yes. If it's money that is stopping you, it wouldn't take much to put up new signs. The furniture is so old, it's almost retro cool. We could leave it alone and play up that aspect in the signage. It's more about the way you frame the business. Do you have a website, socials, and all that?"

"No, I'm a total Luddite." She rolled her eyes. "Of course, I do."

"Cool. We can rebrand. It'll be great."

"Easy for you to say."

He rubbed his forehead. "I don't understand. What is the issue?" She kept pushing his help away. People didn't do that to him. She drew in a deep breath, her perfect tits rising and falling beside him. He caught a whiff of her happy candy scent, at odds with her snarky responses, and he wanted to smile at the contradictions she projected.

"It's family."

"What has that got to do with business?" He blinked at the random answer to his question.

She huffed out an annoyed laugh. "You don't have family, do you? If you did, you wouldn't ask that question."

"No. It's always just been me and Mum."

"Right. So you basically have no idea then?"

"Tell me." He'd always wondered what it would be like to have family. A few of his school friends had big families and he hungered for that easy companionship they had with their siblings, the way they fought and laughed, and stuck by each other. He completely missed out of the whole 'only I'm allowed to hurt my brother' take on life. Like a luxury car, he knew it was a nice to have. He hadn't missed any of the essential stuff growing up, because his mum had worked hard to give him every opportunity. She'd taken the setback to her life that was an unwanted, unexpected pregnancy, and created a life for them both. He knew how goddamned lucky he was to have her. If only his longing for more family didn't make him squirm with guilt. She should be enough family, especially when he was her everything.

"I told you I inherited the business from my Pappous, yeah?"

"Yes. The original Spiro."

"Yeah. Well, to cut a long story short, some of the family didn't agree with his decision and others feel that I should preserve his legacy. And then—" She blew out a long breath. "Then there are my clients. They want what Pappous gave them, none of 'that modern stuff', so it's difficult to even contemplate changes."

"What do you want?"

"Does it matter?"

"Absolutely! You come before family."

"Ha! You definitely have no family if you can say that!" She stared up at the ceiling. Comments like that made his craving for family stronger. Many of his mates, and colleagues spoke with envy of his solo life with the freedom to do anything or anyone. He always smiled and told them, truthfully, they were lucky to have people who cared for them. The freedoms of living solo weren't as thrilling as the longing to belong. Perhaps it all came back to a core feeling of abandonment thanks to his deadbeat father who left before he was even born. He didn't even know the dickhead's name, and the few times he'd asked when he was a kid, his mum pushed him away. If he ever found out who the asshole was, he'd probably shoot him. He'd rather not know. Mum had done everything she could to make him grow up feeling special, her treasure. And he'd forever be thankful to her for seeing him as himself. When he'd discovered his fascination with art history, she'd reminded him to find a practical path. Art won't pay the bills. Keep it as a hobby.

In the end, he'd managed to merge his creativity with money. Together with Vince, they'd started Kapow. Vince with the money and business nous, Stu with the creative ability to sell anything to anyone. Vince had rewarded him with shares in the multi-million dollar business, and Stu used those profits to travel to the world's greatest museums.

"I don't understand why you let your family stifle your ambition." His mum had encouraged him to strive for success, and she'd celebrated every victory alongside him. Front row seats to everything he'd achieved, from the participation medals at soccer when he was five, to his graduation ceremony from Sydney Uni. He thanked her in the most simple of ways, with an investment portfolio that allowed her the freedom to purse her own dreams. Now she didn't have to worry about money, she could travel, and she'd recently decided to learn to play the cello.

"It's hard to explain. You'd have to meet them." Poppy threw a comment out there for Stu to grab, and he grasped it with both hands.

"Okay. When?"

"Oxi Day. It's on Saturday, and we always have a big

celebration. Come to that and meet the Karahalios clan. Then you'll see what I have to consider when making decisions about Pappous' legacy."

"Really? I'd love to come to a family party." He rolled onto her and kissed her full on the lips.

She smiled against his mouth. "I hope you are brave. It'll be a crowd."

"My ability to wow a crowd is not in doubt." His stomach flipped underneath his confident words. If it didn't matter so much, it might be easier. He had an uncomfortable sense that he was about to get an overdose of family, and suddenly, he wasn't sure he was ready. It was time to change the subject. "What's Oxi Day?"

"Oxi means No in Greek. Oxi Day, 28 October, is the day Greece said No to the invading Italian army in World War Two."

"Italy invaded Greece?" Stu's knowledge of modern history was pretty shaky; he knew about the Italian leader Mussolini being an ally with Germany, but that was about the extent of it.

"Mussolini demanded that Greece allow his troops inside our borders, or we would face war. Metaxas said No, and Greece was forced to defend our borders. And not only that, but we won, beating them back into Albania."

"Cool."

"Yeah, I'm especially proud of Pappous and Yiayia. They were only young when the war came to Miko Papigo—that's their village up in the mountains—they both fought."

"I take it Yiayia is your grandmother. She fought too?" Stu's chest swelled with pride on her behalf.

"Yes. The village women carried ammunitions to the fighters, they are quite famous actually, and fed soldiers."

"And came to Australia after the war?" He had no idea what his relatives had done during the war. His mother didn't talk about her parents, and he had no idea who his father was. His genetic ancestors could have been war heroes, although he doubted it. His father had demonstrated his spinelessness before Stu had even taken his first breath.

"Yes. Surry Hills wasn't as exclusive back then. Pappous started working for other people, and eventually was able to buy the shop. He is a hero in our family."

Stu nodded, suddenly understanding her reticence for change. "And that's why you can't make any changes to your business. Because everyone sees it as his legacy."

"Absolutely."

"After I meet them, I'll come up with a strategy." He loved a challenge like this. There must be a way to grow her business and capitalise on the family story. Because it was a cracker of tale.

"Good luck." She slung her arm over his waist, her eyes drifting closed. Once her breathing evened out, he threw a blanket over them both and slowly let sleep consume him.

Stu awoke on Friday morning, the air sultry with the promise of hot summer day. He hadn't bothered to shut the blinds last night, he'd been focused on Poppy, and now the dawn light streamed inside. Poppy lay curled against his side, her delightful curves soft against his harder body. His morning erection begged for more attention, needing more of her. He cursed his past self for waiting so long to ask her on a date. She didn't fit with his lifestyle, and he could already hear the undercurrent of sneers that would occur if he took her to a work party. A competing thought argued in his head; his attraction to Poppy was none of their business. In many ways, their situation didn't require any of this thinking. His career shouldn't be built on which tall, thin, leggy model he had on his arm. After his experience with Jamie, he didn't trust any of them anyway. Damned career climber, only wanting to fuck him to get access to Vince. Vince, whose sexuality was a closely held secret, but more importantly, whose cynicism about people kept the likes of Jamie and her cohorts at bay. Stu blew out a huff at the dichotomy facing him. Wanting someone he could trust and believing it shouldn't matter about appearances didn't make it true. Image mattered in his job, and Poppy didn't fit the image.

"That's a big sigh for so early in the morning." Her voice crackled with sleep, and the husky sound vibrated into his chest.

"Just thinking about work." He hated the split inside him, his drive for success to prove that he wasn't a terrible misfortunate for his mother, and the nagging doubt he felt for desiring someone who didn't fit his career drive. He ground his teeth. Changing Poppy wouldn't solve this, she wouldn't be perfect anymore. If only his idea of perfection matched the world's current image of beautiful. If only his drive to succeed meant being with Poppy could only be temporary.

"What on earth has you growling under your breath?"

He buried his face against her neck, roughly licking the curve over her collarbone. "I want to spend all day in bed with you."

She chuckled and rolled over so their faces met. "You shouldn't say things like that."

"Why not?"

"Today is one of the busiest days at work. I should be there already, not lying here wishing I could make your desires come true."

A wave of heat throbbed through his torso. "Fuck, Poppy. I should be the one showering you in desire." He pressed his lips to hers, using his internal anguish to show her how much he wanted her. He poured every frustration with the world, and every delight he enjoyed about her, into the kiss. Of course, she met him directly, her brown eyes wide and focused on him, as she took what he gave her and demanded more. More passion, more thrills coursing in his chest. He pushed his hands into her silky tresses, her hair spilling over the back of his hands in a reminder of last night. Her hands spread over his back, down until she grabbed his arse and pulled him tighter against her. His cock pressed against her stomach, desperate.

"Poppy." He started to ask for her consent, the insistent question in the back of his brain, created by his dead-beat sire, which he always, always asked, but a tinny electronic buzz broke into his world.

"Is that your alarm?" She squinted over at his bedside table.

"Yeah." He reached over to his phone to press snooze.

"What time is it?"

"Seven."

"Holy shit, Stu. I have to be at work in an hour." Her eyes widened and she scrambled out of bed. He half-followed her, sitting on the edge of the bed to stare at her.

"An hour should be heaps of time. Your salon is only a few streets away."

"Says you. I don't have any other clothes, and I'm sure as heck not going to work all day in last night's undies. Gross." She grabbed her dress and shook it out. He probably shouldn't smile, or want to grab her back into bed, but the way her breasts swayed as she moved hit him in an elemental place where testosterone surged.

"Can't you go home and grab some new clothes?" He could barely make his brain work, all his blood had rushed to his cock as she stood nude in his room with defiance in her stare.

"Not in an hour. Not all of us can afford to live so close to the city." She stormed into his bathroom. He leapt off the bed to follow her as he figured out a solution.

"Poppy, I can buy you new underwear if that's what you need." Anything to absolve himself for daring to think she wasn't enough for his dream life and career.

She spun around, hands on hips. "Before the shops open? That'd be some achievement."

"Hey, how did we get here?"

"A cab?" Sarcasm flowed off her tongue, an effective way to snub out his arousal. A swarm of icicles replaced the happy warmth inside him, and he ran his hand through his hair.

"No, I mean this argument. I don't understand."

Poppy sighed, and the breath hit him in the chest hard. "Of course you don't. You might be able to ignore your responsibilities and swan about in bed with some girl you brought home last night. I can't. The shop must open today. It's one of the busiest days of the year."

"You were willing last night."

"Don't throw that in my face, Stu. I'm allowed to enjoy myself. I'm even allowed to enjoy myself without worrying about the next day."

"I agree. I'm not the one making a big deal of this." Stu heard the defensive note in his voice and tried not to cringe. She bowed her head as a pink flush broke out over her skin, and she crossed her arms over her stomach.

"Look at me, Poppy. We are both adults, who had a wonderful night together. I'm sure we can find a solution to any problem without awkwardness."

She lifted her head and met his gaze, uncertainty written on her face. He stepped towards her, reaching for her hands. He lifted them off her stomach and placed them on his hips.

"Poppy, I'll get you to work on time. I promise."

"Okay." She drew the word out as if she didn't quite trust him. He swallowed. Did she instinctively know the conflict inside him?

"Let me try and solve your problems."

"Hmmm…" Her face contorted half in a glare and something else. He hoped that look meant she might let him try and help her, but she gasped, then waved her hand carelessly. "—Never mind." She gave a half-hearted laugh. "I have a set of spare clothes at the salon. I completely forgot.

They've been sitting in a cupboard out the back for months."

"That's my girl. Solving your own problems." He kissed her before she could argue with him again, and definitely before she might notice his smile and realise that he liked her feisty arguments. She softened against him, sending the icy worry fleeing as desire surged again.

"Come in the shower with me."

"Only if you promise I won't be late."

Stu grinned and kissed her on the forehead. "I wouldn't dare."

9

Poppy pushed open the door to her salon, unable to wipe the smile off her face. Stu was easily the best lover she'd ever had. No wonder she'd wanted to argue with him at every chance, it might be the only way she'd keep him at a distance. She wasn't ready to gift her heart to a man who only wanted a plaything. She fanned her face at the memory of his strong hands soaping her body as they showered together. He'd washed every inch of her skin, from between her toes, the tips of her fingers, behind her ears, and inside her. She'd orgasmed twice in the shower, once as he'd stroked her pussy with lust and attention, her own wetness mixing with the warm shower water, and again when he fucked her up against the wall, his cock buried deep inside and his fingers all slippery and needy against her clit. He'd even wiped up the wet footprints he'd left on the floor when he'd leapt out of the shower to grab a condom. If she wasn't careful, she'd fall hard for his consideration of her needs. Her knees were still weak as she walked inside, right on time. Stu certainly kept his promises, putting her first at every opportunity. No wonder she doubted her ability to keep her heart safe. *Just sex. It was just sex.* Surely if she told herself that phrase often enough, she'd be fine. One night to remember.

"Doing the walk of shame!" Levi cackled as she entered.

"Heck yes." Her smile stretched and broadened.

"He's as good as he looks, then?" Levi had begun the Stu arse appreciation society last year, and the two of them sighed every time Stu walked out of the shop. Her fingers tingled with the knowledge of how good Stu's arse felt under her palms.

"And some."

"Awesome." Levi held his hand up for a high five, and she dutifully slapped it. "I was worried for you."

"Why? I'm an adult."

"Not because of that. It's just that loads of guys with amazing bodies really suck at sex. I'm so glad Stu lived up to the promise of his fucking hot body."

Poppy pressed her tongue against the back of her teeth. "What?"

"Ok. Maybe it's a gay thing, and yes I can say that since I'm gay, but the problem with hot men is they only care about themselves. Which makes them a boring fuck."

"Right—" Poppy drew out the word as she mused on Levi's comment. "Stu's not like that. I mean, he has an arrogance about him, but he—" She swallowed. Levi grinned cheekily, encouraging her to continue.

"—He cared about my pleasure too." Her face burned hot.

"Excellent. I've always had a good feeling about him. I'm glad you are happy, Poppy."

"Thanks. Now should we open up for the day?" Poppy needed a little normality in her day. Levi's friendship mattered to her. They spent all day together, and he had grown to be more than her apprentice. But she wasn't quite ready to analyse last night, and this morning, with Levi yet.

"Yeah, yeah. Did you see the sign I wrote for today?"

"No. What did it say?"

Levi wrinkled his nose and made a tutting sound. "You didn't read my sign. Stu must have been good."

"That's enough now."

"Oh come on." He winked. "Don't go all boss lady on me. You know you can talk to me if you are worried about anything. And no-one is perfect."

Poppy shook her head. "You aren't going to stop until I tell you something, are you?"

"Nope. I'll be here all day, waiting for the perfect gossip." Levi made a pretence of tidying up his already perfectly tidy workstation.

"He talked the whole time. I've never known someone to talk so much."

"Weird."

"Hell no. It was hot." She fanned herself with a piece of paper from the front desk.

"No regrets, then?"

Poppy chewed her bottom lip. "Maybe one?"

"Tell me everything." Levi's eyes lit up at the prospect of good gossip.

She let out a long breath, still unable to believe she'd done this. "I might have, maybe, in a moment of silliness—"

"Come on, you can tell me. I'm sure it's not that bad, unless it's a weird kink thing."

Her whole face blazed at the memory of her hair wrapped around Stu's cock. "It's not a kink thing; which by the way, aren't weird if both people want it. I invited to a family party tomorrow." She scrambled through the last bit.

"Like, with your whole family. The entire Karahalios clan?" Levi's eyes widened in mock horror. Poppy nodded.

"You are right. That was quite the moment of silliness. Although, on the upside, you'll discover how brave he is." Levi giggled.

"Shut up. What about how brave I'll have to be?"

"You. You'll be fine. Imagine all those cousins seething with jealousy when they see you with super hot fake silver fox Stu." Levi winked, and the faint churn in Poppy's stomach stopped. She smiled.

"Oh my God. It's going to be perfect. I'll put up with any amount of 'how did you meet?' 'is it serious?' 'when are you getting married?' and the squeals of 'oh my baby is getting married!' to watch some of the cousins faces when they see him."

"Didn't you tell me that a few of them said that it didn't matter if you got the Surry Hills property, because you'd never get married anyway and they'd end up with it eventually?"

Poppy's shoulders sagged. "Thanks a fucking lot for reminding me. Levi. And yeah, you missed the bit about how no man wants a plump wife, and I'd have to lose some pounds to pick up anyone. Blah blah." She perked up. "Stu seemed pretty happy to be asked." Probably a bit too happy; she wished she could trust that he truly liked her and it wasn't just a one night thing.

"Pretty happy with your shapely curves too. It'll definitely put all that cruelty to bed if you show up with him." No wonder she considered Levi to be a good friend. He knew exactly what to say to make her feel better.

"Hell yeah!" She reached up to high five Levi, their palms slapped and they both grinned. "Now, time to work."

Poppy's feet, knees, and hips ached. She'd been on her feet for over twelve hours, as clients keep pouring through the door. So many cuts, as people prepared for tomorrow's celebrations. She hadn't had a moment to herself. Usually, she was able to do some of the accounts during the day. Not today. She'd be reconciling the day's takings until late into the evening. The joys of owning a small business. She shook her head, this was a good problem to have.

"Time to lock up. I'm off for a Friday Frolic." Levi finished a final sweep up.

"Lucky for some." Poppy smiled at Levi's reference to his favourite nightclub's weekly event. She'd heard plenty about his frolicking at the club.

"Stu hasn't called?"

Poppy half-shrugged. "Honestly, I haven't had time to check my phone all day."

"Do it." Levi's enthusiasm made her smile. All she

wanted was to curl up on the couch, argue with her accounting software for a while, then catch up on the lack of sleep from last night. She smiled as she opened the drawer of the front desk to grab her phone. There was a missed call from Stu, and a text.

Stu: Hey there. What time should I pick you up tomorrow?

The message was time stamped a few hours ago. Poppy rubbed her temple as she calculated.

Poppy: You don't have to come if you don't want. Can you pick me up from the salon at noon?

Her phone dinged with an instant reply.

Stu: Perfect. Do you want a drink tonight? I'm at work drinks. Should be finished soon. Then we can meet somewhere.

Poppy: Nice for some. I've only just finished for the day, and still have the accounts to do.

Stu: Have you eaten?

Poppy's stomach rumbled. Shit, she'd missed lunch. No wonder she felt exhausted, she'd put it down to her late night with Stu. She sat, collapsed, on the shop's waiting couch.

Poppy: It's okay, I'll grab something on the way home.

"Hey, Poppy. Good night. See you in the morning."

"Thanks Levi. Enjoy your night out." She smiled at her apprentice as he bounced out of the door with a cheeky grin. Time to haul herself to her feet before she fell asleep here. Snoozing at work, even now as evening was in full swing, wasn't a great look. Anyone might peer inside and see her. It was unprofessional. She tucked her phone into her shirt pocket, locked the front door, and started to gather up her things. She counted the cash takings, making a note in her record book, and pressed the button that sent a summary of the computer transactions to her email before shutting down the electronic system and unplugging it. Everything got locked into the safe, hidden in the back cupboard, and once locked, an app tracked the location of the safe from her phone. With everything backed up to the cloud for good measure. Pappou would be amazed at the technology. He'd simply walked home each night with the cash takings in his pockets. She locked the cupboard and the back room before a final tidy up. With last night's dress stuffed into a bag, Poppy left work, completing her lockup with the front door key, and walked to the train station.

Surry Hills buzzed with Friday night revellers, all beginning their weekends in style at the many pubs and restaurants lining the streets. Poppy ducked into the kebab place, and ordered her regular lamb kebab, her stomach protesting her lack of lunch loudly. The anticipation of Oxi Day tomorrow, and seeing all the family, made the back of her neck prickle with guilt. Eating Greek food from a shop told the world she was a bad cook, or at least, she'd had that comment drummed into her as a kid. Did she believe that? Not tonight when her feet hurt as she waited, and she stood with her hand pressed into the ache in her lower back. The pain represented income. Poppy blew out a long breath and tried not to worry about Stu meeting her family tomorrow. She tapped her toe in her shoe. Hurry up. Her stomach growled again. Maybe she should have some baklava as well. No, she should cut back on sweets. The guy behind the counter handed her kebab over, and she thanked him before walking to the train station.

A few minutes later, she stood on the platform unwrapping the kebab. The scents made her mouth water as she bit into the soft wrap, tender lamb, and sharp-tasting tabouli. Just what she needed. Comfort food at the end of a long, hard day's work. The train pulled in as she was finishing, and she wiped her mouth on the paper napkin before stepping aboard. Poppy sat in her usual seat and pulled out her phone to spend the next half-hour or so catching up on social media. Oh, and she should email her product suppliers with a new order. She sighed, wanting to put work aside, and read for the next hour. At least work would keep her focused away from Stu. She rested her head against the window, the smooth glide of the train and the montage of the city flashing as the train sped homewards. Stu. Why had she invited him to Oxi Day? He'd said yes and now she couldn't just pretend it was a one time only thing. Filed away in the Stu Arse Appreciation Society folder of her memory. Now there would be awkward family introductions, and questions, so many questions! When did you meet? What does he see in you? Urgh. And the big one: could she guard herself against the hurt when he ended it? She bit her lip. What was she doing worrying about the ending? They'd had one night of fun, with no expectation of more, except she really wanted more, hence the throwaway invitation. If only he'd said no. Damn it. She wound her bright hair around her fingers. That was the crux of it. She wanted more time with him. Now they'd made the leap from client and hairdresser into lovers, she couldn't bear thinking about silently doing his hair if he decided once was enough for him. Ugly memories flooded in, a sinking weight in her guts, as though her dinner was made of concrete.

About a year after Stu had started coming into the salon, Levi had googled him. Seemingly endless photos of him at various advertising awards nights, or in the Social Sydney pages of that silly free commuter newspaper, with Stu and a parade of slim blonde models. Stu obviously had a type, and she wasn't it. She drew a deep breath in through her nostrils and coughed as the dank scent of the train seats came with the air. Poppy refused to play the 'what I wasn't fat' game, she knew that road only led to unhappiness. Thanks to her genetics, she would never be tall and elegant. She shrugged. So what if she was plump? So what if she had brown eyes, a Greek nose, and ever-changing hair. Stu obviously desired her, as evidenced by last night. Besides, if she could accept herself and her body, everyone else could go jump. Tired of the anxious swirl of thoughts, she glanced at her phone for the distraction, only to see a text from him.

Stu: I've finished up here. Where do you want to meet?
Poppy: Can I pass? I'm on the train going home.
Stu: Long day?
Poppy: Non-stop.
Stu: I can drop by yours. I'll bring a bottle of champagne.

Poppy grinned to herself. Why was she doubting this? He'd said yes to Oxi Day, even knowing that her whole big loud Greek clan would be there, and he kept saying yes to her. Why worry about trying to understand this? She would take his yes and enjoy the moment.

Poppy: Forget the champagne, it'll put me to sleep. Tell you what, if you massage my feet, I'm all yours. She blushed, heat prickling her cheeks at her own boldness.

Stu: My hands are yours to command.

Poppy pulse quickened, and anticipation made her fingers slippery on the glass of her phone as she texted her address to him, while silently leaning forward in her seat to encourage the train to transport her home faster.

10

G ood sex made his ideas flow better. Today had been a wonderful example of that, having solved the latest crisis unfolding with one of his big clients. Their CEO had hated the latest TV ads they'd worked up for them, sending both him and Kapow's owner Vince into damage control. This morning, Stu had dropped Poppy off at her salon, and bounced into work with the perfect solution. A couple of frantic meetings, and the whole drama had been solved and toasted with a waterfront lunch with the client. Handshakes all around, and business with them was safe for the next while. His afternoon had been filled with similar successes. Even surly Craig, the creative manager who coveted Stu's job, or more accurately, his close relationship with Vince, had congratulated him. And so he should, it was Craig's teams' screw up that led to the situation in the first place.

Stu strutted out of his ride-share car and up to the old 1930s apartment building in Kogarah. He climbed the stairs, his hands filled with flowers and champagne, and knocked on her door with the back of his hand. The door opened a fraction.

"It's me." Stu peeked into the crack to see white fabric and a flash of Poppy's rainbow hair.

"Oh. Come in." Poppy opened the door properly to let him in, and a sleek tabby cat sidled out of the door, rubbing its body on his leg as it walked past. Poppy wore jean shorts, bare feet, and a white shirt that hung loose over her body. A breeze slipped in with him, and her shirt flattened against her body for a moment, giving him a hint of the red underwear underneath. He paused, half inside the doorway, as his mouth watered at the sight of her curves. Oh, man, he had it bad for her.

"Is that your cat?" He cleared away the croak in his voice.

"Nah, it just thinks it lives here…" She smiled, "I'm joking. Yes, Dread lives here."

"Your cat is called Dread?"

A light blush covered her cheeks. "He has only one eye, so he's actually named Dread Pirate George."

"And you call him Dread for short, not Georgie?" Stu chuckled, amused at her choice. She shrugged, and the fabric of her shirt shifted over her body, a reminder of why he was here. Certainly not to talk about her cat while standing in her doorway with his hands full of gifts.

"I know you said no champagne, so I brought you flowers as well."

Her eyes slid to the side, then back to him. "They are beautiful. You shouldn't have."

"I couldn't arrive empty handed."

"All you needed to bring was your empty hands." Her cheeks flushed pink with arousal, a now familiar colour, and she cleared her throat. "I mean, that's what we agreed."

"Will you punish me for reneging on our agreement?" Stu's chest expanded as she grinned.

"Maybe."

"Perhaps you can whip me with your hair again?"

Laughter burst out of her, her head tipping backwards. "You'd like that too much to be a punishment." Her voice sung, rich and sultry. "Come inside, Stu." Poppy stepped backwards, and he followed her, tugged towards her, connected to her even before he touched her. She turned around to rummage in a small cupboard.

"Here, put those in here with some water, and we can go into the lounge." She took the champagne from him and replaced the bottle with a vase. He smiled at the simple domesticity of her actions, before quickly placing the flowers inside and putting the vase on the bench so his hands were free to touch her.

"Tell me Poppy, how sore are your feet?"

"You have no idea. I've been standing all day today. It was great, because we were so busy, which means I'll be able to pay Levi out of the shop takings for the next few weeks, but oh, man, standing all day sucks."

"Come here." He held out his hands, wide and open, until she stepped into him. He wrapped his arms around her back, pressing into the tight muscles of her lower back.

She groaned. "Yes, there. Oh my God, that's good." He swept his hands up her back, kneading her shoulders.

"And there?"

"Mmm, that's nice, but I hardly ever get sore shoulders. I was taught the benefits of good posture early on. It really helps keep my hands from getting tired too."

He slowly let his hands drift down her back, once again massaging her lower back. Her body softened and sagged against his, little purrs coming from her throat. His hands found her hips, and his fingers dug into the flesh, pressing against the knots caused by her job.

"Oh, yeah, there. That's it." She clutched at his shoulders, her head tipping back. He leaned forwards and kissed her throat, her candy scent surrounding him. Only one action mattered now. He swung her into his arms. Her brown eyes flashed wide open, and she squeaked.

"What are you doing?"

"Your feet are sore. I'm here to fix them. The lounge, or your bed?"

She let out a long happy breath. "Bed. It's that way." She pointed her toe towards an open door on the other side of the small lounge.

"Easy." He carried her through the lounge towards her bedroom.

"How strong are you? You aren't even puffing." Naturally, her incredulous tone made his chest expand even further.

"All those gym sessions where I've pushed myself too hard, were all for this moment."

She raised one eyebrow. "Oh, come on. That's laying it on a bit thick."

"You know, Poppy." He shook his head, as he lay her on her bed. "You really keep me grounded."

She laughed, a full riotous laugh that rocked him through his abdomen. "And you are full of it. Just admit that you go to the gym to keep your perfect image, the masculine silver fox, strong, fit, a career success."

"I don't think you should put me into that box quite so neatly." Stu wanted to hear admiration in her voice, not the sarcasm she used to keep him away from her.

"Is that so?"

"Yeah." He pulled his shirt up, exposing his stomach as he lifted it over his head, and heard her sudden intake of breath as he undressed. The simple sound of her enjoyment broke past her snarky comments. He deliberately slowed his movements, taking his time to slip the shirt over his head and off his arms. Stu flung the shirt to the side, flexing his abdomen on purpose for her. She licked her lips, her gaze sliding over his skin, sending electricity skittering over him.

"Well—" She drew out the word into a long syllable. "—You are here with me. So perhaps you are right. You aren't entirely typical."

"Poppy, there is nothing wrong with you."

"I didn't say there was." She waved her hand languidly at him. "I only hint that I'm hardly a fashionable choice for a career climber who hangs out in the social pages."

"I don't care for fashion."

She laughed, a deeply cynical sound. "Yeah, right. Says the guy who shows up in designer jeans and expensive shirts."

"And gets his hair cut at Surry Hills most unfashionable salon." Stu said, part taunt, partly to illustrate his point, and partly to jump in before she noted that he designed his hair to suit his career ambitions.

She gasped, sitting up on her bed to glare at him. "Touché."

"If you are going to snark at me, you should expect a little in return."

"Only a little. I was promised…" Poppy paused, and his imagination quickly filled the blank, never doubting that she paused deliberately.

"I believe you were promised my hands. Command as you wish, Poppy."

She waggled her toes. "Oh, definitely my feet first."

"Do you have massage oil?"

"No, Stu, I invited you here under the premise of a massage, but I really just want sex. It's my secret plan!" Her smile stretched, and he barked out a laugh as she pointed to her bedside table. A bottle of coconut massage oil sat next to a pile of hair-dressing magazines and a couple of condoms. Her half-empty packet of birth control pills lay casually beside a bottle of perfume.

"Right. I see you have everything organised. No wonder you can run a small business, you have the necessary skills to keep things running smoothly."

"Stu, I don't need your vague flattery—"

He grinned. "Rubbish. Everyone loves to be flattered."

She lifted her feet up in the air, and his gaze followed the line of her bare legs, down to the cut-off jean shorts covering her arse. Her breasts jiggled under her flowing shirt as she wiggled her legs, still laughing. Her shirt caught under her back and a flash of round skin showed above her shorts.

"—Then you should flatter my sore legs. I've been working my arse off all day in the business you seem so obsessed with."

He leaned over and pressed a kiss to her stomach, then knelt on the end of her bed, and grabbed her feet, settling them on his legs. Her lips parted on a gasp as he held her ankles tight. Her soft skin in his hands seared him, sending a shock of heat into his chest. Filthy thoughts filled his head as he stared along the length of her body stretched out before him. It would so easy to flip her onto her stomach, rip her already ripped shorts off, and pump himself inside her bountiful body. Her soft round arse full in his hands. But he wanted a willing partner. And for that he would wait.

"Are you alright?" Poppy pushed herself up on her elbows, reaching up with one hand to press a finger between his eyebrows.

"Yeah." He leant forward and kissed her, a gentle reassurance, for his sake more than hers. "Let me show you my magic hands. In a couple of hours, your aches will be replaced with—"

"—an ache of a better sort?" The way she switched between teasing and sarcasm intrigued him.

He pressed a hard kiss to her lips. "Pass me the oil." Poppy lay back on the bed, twisting to the side as she reached for the bottle of massage oil on her bedside table. Her shirt pulled tight over her body, giving him a glimpse of her gorgeous breasts, before she rolled back and handed him the bottle. He took it from her, skimming his fingers over the back of her hand, enjoying the way she shivered. Stu slid the cool bottle up the inside of her thigh towards her feet.

"Stu…" Poppy breathed out his name as gooseflesh broke out on her thighs.

"Yes?" He raised one eyebrow, keeping his gaze firmly on hers, while he pumped the bottle to spurt oil onto her ankles. She closed her eyes, a long slow blink, pink splashed over her face. Stu dropped the bottle on the bed and started to massage her feet. Long strokes to spread the oil over her skin, then firmer on the pads of her feet. She groaned.

"Like that?" He rolled his thumb over her arches, and her only response was a quiet hum. Satisfaction made his chest expand. Having slaked his lust yesterday with her, he had more control tonight, and wanted to make her tremble and moan and beg for him. He worked on one foot at a time, stroking each muscle, coaxing each sore point into relaxation. Slowly he explored, figuring out where she hurt, watching her face for the wince, and every time he massaged a tight muscle, she would moan. Her sounds sung directly into his cock, like a siren singing to his erection, until he strained at his pants and had to shift on the bed to ease the pressure.

"Roll over." He gripped her hips, helping her flip over. "Yeah, that's it. And stretch out. Put your hands above your head."

"Like this?" Poppy complied with his order. Fuck yeah, like that!

"Do you trust me?" He knew the answer would be yes, so when she rolled her head to stare at him, he frowned and leaned away from her.

"Stu. I invited you into my house and am now lying prone on my bed at your command." The sultry way she said command made his heart race. "This is the very picture of trust."

"Excellent. Take off your clothes."

"While lying face down on my own bed?" Poppy questioned his command.

"Yes. I want to see you wriggle. And if you argue again, I will find a way to keep you quiet."

She half-sat up on her elbow, and grinned. "Will you put your dick in my mouth?"

"God, Poppy." He swallowed. Thoughts of kissing her to stop her talking fled, replaced with a more salacious image. "Maybe later. Now lie down and get nude."

Her grin expanded. "As you wish." Hot damn, her cheeky responses were everything. She plumped the pillow, before laying down as he requested, her face hidden from him, and her colourful hair spread around her head. His fingers tingled with the need to stroke her hair, but he wasn't sure she would want massage oil on the long strands. Instead, he flicked open his own jeans, and tugged them down. She wriggled on the bed as she wrestled with removing her shirt. Now nude, he held his cock in his oily hands, as she won the battle over her shirt and flung it away. She reached behind her back, and flicked open the bra, the red straps pinging wide, leaving behind pink marks on her skin where the tight elastic dug into her.

"Leave it." He wanted to see the bra over her breasts later. She nodded and traced her hands down her sides.

"Minx." He growled out, as she teased him at his own game. Her hands slipped under her stomach, and her hips and arse rose up as she undid her jean shorts. He stroked his cock, his gaze glued to her round lush arse cheeks as she writhed on her bed in the act of removing her clothes. She started to push them down her legs, leaving her lacy red underwear behind. He knelt over her legs, trapping them under his naked thighs, and gently took her hands off her clothes. Her jean shorts around her knees kept her trapped beneath him.

"That'll do now." He moved her hands back above her head, then spread his hands over the marks left by her bra, gently stroking his oily hands on her skin to soothe her. Stu leaned forwards, stretched over her back, and licked the top of her ear. His cock throbbed as it pressed against her arse. He had to suck in a deep breath to fight the urge to fuck her right this moment. If pleasure was a currency, she had two years of debt to pay. Two years of little touches to his scalp, each reaching down inside him. Every moment of pleasure she'd given him, he would give back until she screamed his name in desperate release. He sat up, dragging his hands roughly down her back. Only the residual oil on his palms made the action smooth. Stu skirted his hands over her arse, and Poppy responded with breathy pants. He grabbed her underwear and shorts, shifting so he stood at the end of the bed, and a quick tug was all it took to slid them down her legs and off. Poppy inhaled sharply, as the fabric left a rough red mark on her skin. Stu grabbed the massage oil bottle and poured it over her legs. He worked it into her calf muscles with long strokes to sooth the marks left by removing her jean shorts, and to ease the ache in her muscles caused by her job. Her thighs trembled with need, and his favourite sound, her little purrs of satisfaction filled the air, muffled by the bed. He knelt between her legs, pushing them apart, giving him the perfect view of her. Soft, pink, wet. Any doubt about her desire fled as she lifted her hips and opened herself up to him more.

"Poppy, you are so fucking gorgeous." He stroked her thighs, long muscle deep strokes to massage her. He pushed his thumbs into those spots on her hips that she'd said were sore earlier.

She groaned. "So good."

Smugness made him smile as he pressed deep circles with his thumbs into her aches. Another long stroke of his palms up her thighs, this time along her inner thigh where the skin was softer, more sensitive than the rest of her. She purred, lifting her hips again, as he skimmed his fingers along the edge of her vulva. Teasing her. With more deep strokes, he massaged her arse muscles, occasionally drifting between her legs to taunt her, until her fingers clenched the bed sheets, and her moans came faster and faster.

"Stu. Please. Fuck me." Her plea roared in his ears, engorging his already thick and ready cock. He shook his head.

"Not yet." His voice growled deep, as he shifted between her legs until his mouth covered her. The coconut from the oil filled his senses, mixing with her own feminine musk, as he flicked his tongue over her clit. She screamed into the pillow, the sound muted by the fabric. He sucked and drank her, fucking her with his tongue as she came, clenching around him, until he could take no more. He grabbed a condom and sheathed himself.

"Now I will fuck you. If you ask nicely." He held the

broad head of his erection at her entrance. She shifted, trying to impale herself.

"No. Ask." He placed one hand in the middle of her back, keeping her in place. Keeping himself in place.

"Please. Stu."

"Ask properly." He slid inside a little way, then out again, gritting his teeth as her body begged for him with a tremble of her arse.

"Fuck me now. Please. Hard and fast."

He slammed inside and she screamed his name as she clenched around him. So tight and wet.

"More." She lifted her head, enough to drag in air as she writhed before him. He reached up for her hair, twisted it around one hand, as he pumped inside, the other hand wrapped around her. Words fled, as she raised her chin up on her elbows, her back bent and her arse in the air as he pounded deep into her.

"Up on your knees." Gravel made his command guttural as he pulled her hair, and she complied. Her breasts dangled as she knelt on her hands and knees with his cock buried inside her. He released her hair, as he slipped both hands around her to cup her breasts while slowing his pace. Her bra lay discarded on the bed beneath her, the perfect symbol of his control and her disarray. Her nipples were hard on his palms, and when he pinched them, she came again, squeezing his cock until his own sweet, sweet release came. Stu collapsed onto her back, and together they lay on the bed, cradled against each other. He had just enough energy left to deal with the condom and to kiss her before drifting into a post-coital snooze.

11

A half-bitten back curse floated into Stu's conscious, and he rolled over to open one eye. The faint pre-dawn light hit the back of his eyeball and he stretched out. His hand brushed against a wooden bedhead, and soft pillows. Holy hell, he'd slept the night at Poppy's house. After the best sex of his life. He sat up and reached for his phone. What the hell was the time? Oh, not even six am yet. A sugary orange smell filled the air as his sense slowly awakened. What was Poppy doing at this ridiculous hour? Stu swung out of bed and wandered into the lounge. The one-eyed cat brushed against his leg, and he reached down to pat it.

"Good morning, Dread." He straightened to see Poppy in the kitchen.

"Good morning to you too." Poppy's gaze flicked over his naked body, causing a stir in his groin. "I see some parts of you wake up before others." Her voice sounded way too cheerful, and Stu rubbed his eyes.

"What on earth are you doing?"

She shook her head, as if her actions were completely obvious. "I'm cooking. Today is Oxi Day, remember."

"Um, yeah? But I don't see why that means you should be cooking at…" He glanced at his phone again, "quarter to six."

"I can't arrive with nothing, and someone—" She gave him a pointed look and cleared her throat. "Someone took up all my spare time last night."

"An excellent use of time."

Her cheeks flushed pink. "Yes. However, the downside is that Revani cakes must be cooked now."

"Must? When does the party start?" Stu still didn't see her logic.

"Stu. As nice as it would be to swan about all morning, making cakes, and getting ready, the salon is open from nine till twelve, and the party starts at one. I'll probably be late, and then I'll have to hear all about how there is more to life than work, and why can't I find a nice boy to look after me."

Stu blinked, then smiled slowly. He spread his arms out in front of him, enjoying the way her eyes tracked his body. "I don't think a nice boy would suit you. He wouldn't be able to give you what you desire."

Her eyebrows shot upwards, and the pink on her cheeks darkened. "And what exactly do I desire?"

Me. Stu let his smile turn predatory. "A real man who will celebrate your work, soothe your aches, and fuck you dirty and hard."

"That does sound ideal." Poppy's voice went husky, the

sound travelling deep inside him, all the way to his cock. Her gaze dropped, spearing him with ready heat.

"Ideally, you'll come back to bed now."

Poppy chewed on her bottom lip.

He wanted to kiss the little bite better. "Come on now, it's an easy decision."

She took a step towards him, her breasts loose under her massive saggy old t-shirt, then stopped. "Give me a minute. I need to get these in the oven, and then you'll have thirty minutes." She made the time limit sound like a dare, and he swallowed.

"I like a challenge." He walked closer to her kitchen and leaned over the bench. "What are you making?"

"Revani cakes. They are basically semolina flour cakes, with a citrus sugar syrup poured over the top. Normally, you'd make one cake, then slice it, but I'm making smaller cup-cake sized ones with orange syrup."

"Because?" Wouldn't one cake be easier, especially this early in the day? Stu cocked his head to the side as he tried to understand her illogical decision.

"Because small cakes look cooler. I'm baking them into shaped moulds as well."

"That seems incredibly complex for this time of day."

"I guess so." She sighed. "It's a Greek thing."

He raised one eyebrow. "What? Complicated ideas before dawn?"

Poppy giggled, and the sound rushed over his skin. Boy, he was absolutely gone for her.

"No, food. Food is a sign of love and dedication. If I

bring a simple cake to lunch, Mama will think that I don't care enough for the family."

"Therefore you deliberately drag yourself out of bed to make individual cakes in special shapes, just to prove your love to your family?" Stu adored the concept, not just of family, but the practical way of showing how much they'd cared for each other, and it settled like a warm blanket around his shoulders.

"Pretty much. These cakes will give the impression that I spent hours making them, which is true. I have spent hours making them. And everyone will know how much time I've dedicated to them. The people, not the cakes. It's a symbol."

Stu smiled. "I get it. It's amazing." A yearning to have that time expended on him, and to belong to a family who treated each other like that, burned inside. Like hot coffee on his tongue, scalding, desirable, and a little bitter because he didn't have it. Yet. Poppy grinned back at him, a wide satisfied smile, as she started to pour the cake mix into the little metal moulds she had laid out on the bench. He watched her hands, competent and strong, as she created. The number of cake moulds seemed to go on and on, and he started to count them.

"You are making thirty-six cakes?"

"Yeah. It's probably not enough, but I only have thirty-six moulds." A tiny hint of self-doubt infused her voice, and he wanted to reassure her.

"How many people are you expecting to feed?" Maybe he should rethink coming with her today. He ran his hand through his hair. Nah, a bigger crowd would be easier than a small gathering. There'd be less time for awkward questions.

Less time for them to discern that he was much more invested in Poppy, than she was in him.

"It's Oxi Day—" She shrugged one shoulder, as if that answer told him everything.

"So?"

"So it'll be all of my family, the extended family, and anyone else who anyone might know."

"Like me?"

"Yeah." She smiled. "Like you. The more the merrier." Poppy put the empty bowl in the sink and started to place the half-filled cakes onto trays. She picked up the first one and turned to put it in the oven. As she bent over, her shirt rose up, giving him the perfect view of her completely nude bottom. His fingers clenched white on the edge of the bench. If he'd known she wasn't wearing anything under that old shirt, he would have taken her right there, over the oven in her kitchen. Risk of being burned, be damned. She spun around and took another tray, repeating the action. This time she bent a little lower, increasing his view of her glistening sex. A noise emerged from the back of his throat.

"Are you alright, Stu?"

"Gah." He coughed. "You are…" perfectly fuckable.

She licked her lips, and sparks flew in his vision, stealing his breath. "Only two more trays to go in, and you are all mine." She knew. His nostrils flared in anticipation. His gorgeous Poppy knew exactly how she affected him, and he wanted to glory in the knowledge, and punish her for tempting him. All at the same time. He couldn't take his eyes off her, as she calmly put cakes into the oven. Her old shirt hung loose on her delightful body. It should have detracted from the soft curves underneath, instead, the flimsy fabric emphasized her curves, and made him want to rip it off her and pound into her. She shut the oven door and lifted her gaze to meet his.

"Fifteen minutes."

"You said thirty." Although if she bent over again in that damned ugly shirt, he wouldn't last five minutes.

"I need to swap the trays over in fifteen minutes, so the bottom ones don't burn." She sounded so sensible, when his own pulse raced wildly, and his hands twitched with greed for her flesh.

"You'd better come here then."

Poppy walked around the kitchen bench into the lounge. Her breasts swayed deliciously under that sloppy shirt, and every step shifted the hem, flashing her dark curls, dragging his attention down her bare legs.

Poppy paused a few steps from Stu as he leaned on the bench, completely nude. Her gaze flicked over his muscled body, as a fresh wave of amazement filled her stomach. No wonder she woke up in a panic this morning and did anxiety baking. He was right. Thirty-six individual cakes was something of an overkill. Men like him, handsome as sin and completely in control of their domains, didn't end up nude in her apartment. Men like him didn't agree to come to a family gathering. Her nostrils flared. Yeah, that was the reason for her insane baking frenzy this morning. Somewhere, somehow, in a very short space of time, Stu had gone from a fuck buddy to meeting her family. She hadn't expected him to agree to come, she'd only asked as a joke. Holy shitballs. She pressed her hands into her stomach. This wasn't a few butterfly nerves inside her, this was a full-blown hornet nest of an argument buzzing in her gut. Introducing him to her clan didn't bother her, at least, not much. What really made her worry was what came next. What would she say to her family when he didn't come to the next party? She didn't expect anything long term from him. She only wanted a bit of fun, deserved fun, after working so hard on maintaining Pappous' business and making it hers. Mama, and all the aunts, wouldn't understand.

"How long until the cakes burn?" Stu's voice dragged her back to the present and Poppy realised she'd been staring at his bare feet. At least when this fling was over, she'd have some amazing memories to hold tight. One day, when she finally succumbed to family pressure and married a nice Greek boy, she'd be able to remember that time she fucked Stu on the floor of her lounge.

"I told you already." A slow smile tugged at her lips.

"What's stopping you then?"

She shook her head, blowing out a short breath. "Nothing much." His comment grounded her worries. They both agreed this was just sex, a fun fling. She lifted her chin and stripped off her old shirt, tossing it away. Stu sucked in a sharp breath between his teeth, and her smile grew. He liked what he saw, that much was certain from the way his steely blue eyes darkened, scorching her freshly bared skin with his lust-filled gaze.

"What do you want, Poppy?" His question sent a wave of heat over her skin, and his nostrils flared in response.

"I—" She cleared her throat. Could she ask for her ultimate fantasy? Him tied to her bed as she explored every inch of him with her tongue. She opened her mouth to suggest it, when Dread leapt between them and pushed his head against her shin.

"Damned cat." Stu reached down to pick up Dread, and Poppy's heart melted as he cuddled her cat in his arms. Dread purred so loudly that Poppy felt a twinge of jealously. She wanted to lie against Stu's chest, although in her fantasy, she wouldn't be resting. She'd comb her fingers through his chest hair, flick her tongue over his nipples, and taste his skin.

She held out her hands for Dread, unable to suppress a grin. "He's probably just hungry. I normally put out some breakfast for him about now."

"Cats before lovers then?" Stu laughed. She glanced away quickly, not wanting Stu to see the truth. Dread would be here with her long after Stu had moved on.

"I can feed you breakfast too." She swallowed back the annoying twinge of hurt and tried to sound as cheerful as possible. He would move on, and that would have to be okay. She'd agreed to some fun, nothing else. She wouldn't get hurt if she didn't let herself get too close to him.

"That'd be great." His stomach grumbled, the rough sound mingling with Dread's ridiculously loud purrs. Poppy turned away from the sight of Stu cuddling her cat, to grab her discarded shirt. God. Could anything be hotter than a man gently holding a cat in his arms? She wanted to fan her burning cheeks, or better, to slide her fingers over her already soaking pussy. A laugh bubbled out at the double entendre as she leaned over to pick up her shirt. Sensation slammed through her, turning the laugh into a guttural moan, as Stu stepped behind her, his hard cock pressed up against her exposed arse.

"Poppy." His voice rumbled through her body. He was so close against her, that the rough hair on his thighs pushed against her softer legs, abrading her senses. "Forget about breakfast. I'll eat you instead."

Her knees softened. Hell, yes. She spread her legs wider, unable to talk, as he sank down. His abdominal muscles grazed her arse cheeks, and she trembled as he paused to put Dread on the ground beside them.

"You know he's going to wind himself around us until I feed him." She managed to say as Stu stroked his large hands over her back. Stu pressed a hard kiss to the base of her spine, and his hands skimmed over her hips, until they wrapped around her.

"Dread is welcome to try and distract me." His words blew over her exposed slit, cool on her hot, slick sex as he continued to sink to his knees behind her. She only knew he knelt because his body still touched her legs and his shape was tattooed onto her skin. He gently pushed her feet wider, settling between them.

"Say yes, Poppy."

"Yes." Poppy reached out for the back of the couch, needing something solid to hang onto as Stu's tongue flicked out against her pussy. Blood rushed to her head, dizzy as she bent over for him. Her moans built, becoming frantic as his mouth covered her. Her thighs trembled. Her breathed raced, emitting little pants, as Stu sucked and licked her sodden body. His tongue found her clit and she cried out. Power and vulnerability overwhelmed her as his mouth covered her, suckling on her juices, until her head thrashed, her moans erratic with pleasure. With his thumb toying with her hard, swollen nub of nerves, wave after wave of sensation spun through her body, until she begged him for more. She opened herself up, bending further, until she breathed so hard and fast she thought she might hyperventilate. He slid his tongue inside her, and she clenched around him, bucking against his face. Primitive and raw. Her legs weakened completely, and still, he held her strong, lapping at her with his mouth as pleasure coursed over her until her cries became breathless pants of glory. He scorched her so much she could smell burning.

"Oh, shit. The cakes." Her voice sounded drugged, as she struggled to drag her boneless body back into the real world. Stu bounced to his feet, wrapping his arms around her waist to help her find her footing. His hard cock pressed against her, and she wanted to let the cakes burn.

"Shall I turn the oven off?" Stu asked.

She shook her head, as she tried to clear the happy fog of pleasure. "No, I'll do it. I need to change them around, so they cook evenly." Poppy reluctantly stepped out of his arms, and back into the real world. The world where spectacular orgasms were rare. The world that demanded her time in return for a sense of independence. She tossed on her shirt and paced the few steps back to the kitchen. With a couple of oven mitts, she pulled out the bottom tray, placed it onto the stovetop, and slid the top tray down to the bottom. A few more rearrangements, and every tray had a new shelf. Poppy grabbed a clean knife and tested a couple of cakes on each tray. None came out clean, and she hoped they would cook through without burning the base. She closed the oven, double checked the temperature. No, it wasn't too hot, they should be okay. And all the while, Stu's gaze burnt into her back, bringing her wrung out body sparking back to life for another round.

"Dread, come here lad." She called out to the cat, who bounded into the kitchen with a scowl. "Yes, I know, it's later than usual. I've been distracted." She glanced up at Stu who shrugged his shoulders.

"Poor kitty, I guess he's not used to being second in your life."

Had she imagined the undertone that hinted his desire to be number one in her life? She hoped not. Down that path lay disaster, heartbreak and upset. She knew better than to trust her instincts over a man's heart. Desire, she understood. Love, no. She'd been burnt on that road before. Trusting too easily. Poppy ignored Stu's comment, unable to come up with a response that didn't give away her feelings. Instead, she pulled open the cupboard, and poured out some dried food for Dread. She stepped towards the fridge, the cool rush of air being exactly what her over-heated imagination and body required. She grabbed the container of fresh lambs fry she'd cut up for Dread yesterday and spooned out half into Dread's bowl.

"Do you need a lift to the salon this morning?" Stu leaned over the bench, his arms loose and relaxed, as she busied herself with throwing together a quick breakfast for them.

"No. I usually take the train. It's only forty minutes, door to door."

"I took a cab here last night, and it'll be no drama to share one this morning with you if that's easier for you?"

She pursed her lips, as she poured cereal into two bowls for them. "Yeah, traffic isn't too bad on a Saturday morning. That could work."

"I'll pick you up from the salon at twelve, and we can go to the party together."

She blinked slowly. "Yeah, alright." His plan meant she might actually arrive on time, massively reducing the chance of Mama being upset. "I'll return the favour sometime." A frown flashed over his face.

"You don't need to count favours with me. That's not how this works."

"How does it work, then?" She raised her eyebrows as she passed his bowl to cereal to him. He put the bowl on the bench and spread his arms wide.

"No, don't bother. This is just fun. I know that." Poppy didn't need to hear his excuses, or worse, to hear him promise a future that couldn't happen. This fling couldn't last. They came from different worlds; the executive and the hairdresser. Most people in his circle saw her as a servant, doing a lowly job with no formal qualifications, or at least not on the scale that mattered to them.

"Fun is not about counting. Unless you are an accountant or a mathematician, presumably, they enjoy counting. I don't want to you feel like you need to worry about that stuff. I'll drive you today because it's the pragmatic solution to your time issue. In a different circumstance, we'll make the most practical decision again. And whether that's me driving you, or you doing something for me, I don't want to end up in a tit for tat situation."

None of Stu's speech helped quiet the growing anxiety in Poppy's gut about Stu. On the surface it all sounded sensible. Was it wrong that a tiny part of Poppy's heart leapt in hope at the idea of a long-term relationship with Stu? Yeah, definitely wrong. Deep down, she knew a couple of intense nights didn't make a relationship. Dread might think so, but he'd like anyone who stroked his fur. She shouldn't trust her cat to judge character. She ate her cereal, crunching the muesli between her teeth as the cool milk soothed her tongue, and washed away the dry nerves in her mouth.

"Do you agree?"

"Yeah, sure." She glanced up at the clock. "It's time to get these cakes out. Why don't you have a shower while I make the syrup?" There should be just enough time for her to have a shower after she'd finished baking.

"How about I watch you cook, then we shower together?"

She grinned. "Alright, but you can't make me late for work."

12

After a busy morning at work, Poppy stepped through the open front door of the plain brick house she'd grown up in and walked towards the kitchen. Nothing much had changed since she'd left home a decade ago, and the kitchen still held the heart of this home. Conversation buzzed in both English and Greek. Poppy grinned as she heard voices talking over each other, exclamations, and all the usual noise that came with several aunts preparing enough food to feed the Karahalios clan.

"Calliope! I'm so glad you could make it." Poppy's cousin Effie stepped into the hallway and grabbed her in a wild hug, swinging air kisses.

"Great to see you too Effie. It's been an age."

"And who is this?" Effie tilted her chin in Stu's direction.

"Stu Cooper." Stu stuck out his hand for Effie to shake, and she pulled him in for a cheek to cheek welcome kiss. Poppy grinned as Stu coped better than she'd expected.

"We'll have to catch up later. I need to get these cakes to

Mama." Poppy lifted her arms, to show the two big bags she was carrying. Stu had offered to carry them from the car. What did it say about her that she didn't want to trust him with the task of ensuring the cakes arrived in perfect condition? Or perhaps, what did it say about family expectations, and the discussion she knew would happen as soon as they met Stu. The first man she'd introduced to the family.

"Sure, sure. We have plenty of time." Effie's bubbly comment broke into her thoughts and she leaned back against the wall to allow her cousin to squeeze past. Poppy pulled in a long breath to prepare for joining the chaotic sounds pulsing out of the kitchen.

"Who is Calliope?" Stu asked.

"Me. Poppy is a nickname, short for Calliope."

"Cute."

"Cute? Calliope is the muse of heroic Greek poetry."

"No need to get defensive." Stu smiled and brushed his lips against her ear as he whispered, "you certainly inspire me towards poetic thoughts."

Poppy shook her head and swallowed back a hysterical giggle as Stu wooed her while she readied herself for the big introduction. She stepped into the kitchen, and placed her bags filled with perfect little Revani cakes onto the table. A few other items had to be shoved aside and piled up to make room. Poppy knew the moment Stu followed her into the room, as all conversation stopped.

"Mama, this is Stu." Poppy quietly introduced him without any fanfare. Judging by the stares on the five other faces in the room, Poppy knew she had about fourteen seconds to say anything before the room exploded into questions. She leaned her back against the table, twisting her shirt in her fist.

"Calliope, you didn't mention you were bringing someone." Mama jumped in first.

"My apologies for the lack of notice." Stu smiled.

"The more the merrier." Mama waved her hand. Poppy concentrated on taking her cakes out of their containers and arranging them on the platter she'd brought.

"Why don't you go out the back and have a beer with the blokes?" Mama's suggestion was compounded by her aunts and cousin's agreement. Stu didn't immediately respond and when Poppy glanced over at him, the awkward look on his face spurred her into action.

"That's probably for the best."

Stu slipped his arm around her waist and whispered in her ear. "Are you sure?"

"Yes, they want to quiz me about you. I'll be fine. This is normal." She gave him a half-hearted push towards the back door, and he nodded slowly before leaving the room. As she expected, the room exploded with questions.

"How long has that been going on?"

"Why didn't you tell me you were bringing someone?"

"He's quite hot."

"He's old." Mama's voice rang over the top of everyone, and Poppy felt sharp prickles of heat on her cheeks. She wasn't precisely sure how old Stu was, only that she gave him the greying temples that made him look older than his actual years. An unusual silence fell on the room. A short lived silence.

"He must be pushing 40."

"Is he married?"

Poppy shook her head. She wasn't one hundred percent certain and her stomach churned. She couldn't go through that again. No, Stu wasn't like that at all. The questions didn't stop.

"What is wrong with him if he's got so old without marrying?"

"Calliope, what are you thinking? He's not suitable." Goddamned Aunt Maria, always so judgemental on issues she knew nothing about.

"Why can't you go out with Christo's friend? You know, George, he works in scaffolding, and he's the same age as your brother. Much more suitable." Mama's scold made Poppy scowl. George was much more Greek than Stu too. That snippet didn't need to be said, it was written on every face in the room. Unfortunately for George he had the same name as her cat. Poppy opened her mouth to respond…

Aunt Christina's sneer was louder than her comment. "I just don't understand the attraction of an older man."

"More experienced and mature." Yia-yia spoke for the first time, a quiet sly statement from the corner of the room. Poppy's cheek flooded with heat at the implication and the knowing stare from her maternal grandmother.

"He's not old." Poppy cleared her throat. "He's about the same age as me, it's only his prematurely grey hair makes him look older." She skirted around their secret about his faked silver fox look.

"I hope that's not the only place he's premature." Aunt Elena guffawed loudly.

"Shoosh now, Elena. Can't you see you are embarrassing Calliope?" Yia-yia raised one eyebrow.

"She ought to be embarrassed, bringing him here. He looks positively ancient, and Calliope's ridiculous rainbow hair makes her look about sixteen. Talk about a May to December match." Aunt Maria's disdain should have been easy to dismiss, except it hit that spot of doubt in Poppy's head. Again. She steadied her quickening breath. Stu was nothing like Jean-Phillipe. Jean-Phillipe who had made her so many promises when she'd been eighteen, naïve, and in her first apprenticeship. Jean-Phillipe who, she later found out, made those same promises to all his apprentices to lure them into his bed. What she'd learned was that she wasn't special, and older men couldn't be trusted. Jean-Phillipe's only criteria was innocence, and he'd taken pleasure in ruining her trusting view of the world.

"I'm not embarrassed." Poppy spoke clearly, aiming her comment at Mama and pointedly ignoring mean old Aunt Maria. She was mad, and her face probably showed it if the heat in her cheeks was any sign. "Why would I be embarrassed to bring a handsome, young man to a family party?" With the emphasis on young, even though she wasn't wholly certain. "If I was ashamed of him, or of us, I wouldn't have asked him here."

Yia-yia cackled from her corner, while Mama pursed her lips and shook her head.

"I don't know, Poppy. Why haven't we heard about him before today?"

"I'm an adult, Mama. I don't always share my life with you."

"And no wonder, if you all subject her to this interrogation," Yia-yia said. Poppy huffed out a snide little laugh. Yeah, pretty much. Besides, it was probably better to let them all think Stu had been in her life for more than… She blinked. Shit, only since Thursday. Or for two years, if you count the time he'd sat in her chair at the salon. Two days or two years?

"Mama, I've known Stu for a couple of years." Poppy picked the option that would cause the least amount of outcry.

"Two years! For two years, you have been hiding this young man from us. No wonder you have shoved aside my gentle suggestions of nice Greek men. What else don't you tell your Mama?"

Poppy tried not to roll her eyes. "Mama, we haven't been —" She paused as she struggled to find a description of her fast and furious fling with Stu, "—romantically involved for all that time. I'm not hiding anything from you."

"Two years!" Mama wailed dramatically and waved her knife in the air. The scent of freshly chopped parsley wafted in the air.

"Mama…" Poppy began cautiously, as Aunt Christina took the knife from Mama and wrapped her arm around Mama's shoulders.

"Maybe just listen to Poppy about this one. She wouldn't have asked him here to meet you unless it mattered." Christina's calm voice seemed otherworldly among the tension in the air.

"How can it matter when I've never been told? You can't just turn up here with some random guy more than ten years your senior and pretend it's okay. Where is your sense of family duty?"

Poppy glanced at Yia-yia, who grinned in the same way one does when watching a telly-drama unfold. She ignored the jib about Stu's age, after all, he asked to look that way, and concentrated on the question she could answer.

"Every day I care for Pappou's legacy by running his salon in the same way he wanted it. My loyalty to family shouldn't be under question."

"Is he Greek?" Aunt Maria asked her question with the subtly of an elephant, knowing that she was throwing Poppy under a bus. Stu had never mentioned his family, except to say that he envied hers, which was precisely why he was here, and why she bore the brunt of these questions about him. '*I have no idea*' wasn't going to be an answer that would be well received.

"Pappou often said that being Greek was an attitude." Poppy shrugged off Maria's taunt. She sighed, knowing that Mama only asked the questions because she wanted Poppy to be happy. There were worse problems than a loving family who cared about her. The real question revolved around whether Stu would measure up to family expectation. Could she trust him, or would this be just another fling?

"I'm going out to say hi to Papa. Is there anything you want me to carry outside to the BBQ?" Poppy walked to her Mama, kissed her on the cheek, and whispered, "Thank you for caring about me."

S tu smiled as Poppy walked towards the group of men clustered around the BBQ. Her long dark blue skirt swirled around her calves, reminding him of the way he'd nuzzled up against them this morning. Even having her cat headbutt his legs, and beg for breakfast, hadn't stopped him from tasting Poppy this morning. He smiled at her, as her white shirt billowed in the light breeze of the backyard. The simple colours of her outfit made her hair stand out, the bright rainbow bouncing around her face. After introducing himself to the men in Poppy's family, he'd endured plenty of good-natured ribbing from them. Stu left the group, drawn towards Poppy, only to find her brother Christo walking beside him.

"I can see the way you are looking at my sister. If you break her heart, I'll break you." Christo pulled out the protective brother statement in a low undertone as they continued to walk away from the others.

"Mate, she's not fucking fifteen. She can look after herself without you posturing on her behalf. Besides she's more likely to break my heart, than the other way around." Stu enjoyed the sudden blink on Poppy's brother's face, as if he wasn't certain whether Stu had fallen deep for Poppy, or if he was just bullshitting him. Stu's chest tightened as he realised the truth in his comment.

"All the same…"

"Look, mate." Stu tried to slow his racing pulse. "Don't you know your sister at all? If I break her heart, you won't need to break me. She will have already done it."

"Done what?" Poppy's gaze flicked between him and her

brother as they all met in the middle of the yard. "Christo, what have you done?"

Christo held his hands out in the classic soccer playing appealing the umpire gesture. "Hey, come on, Pops. I've done nothing. I'm just reminding your boyfriend here that you have a big family who will protect you."

Stu kept his face as neutral as possible, although his heart skipped a beat when Christo said boyfriend.

Poppy laughed and punched her brother in the arm. "I don't need your old fashioned protection. I'm perfectly capable of looking after myself."

Stu smirked. "Told ya."

"Hmmm…" Christo ignored his jest, and focused on Poppy. "You are certainly braver than me."

"Always have been—" Poppy smiled, then her mouth dropped open. "Why do you say that?"

Christo raised his eyebrows. "You invited your boyfriend to Oxi Day without telling anyone. Did you get absolutely grilled inside?"

Poppy's nose crinkled, and Stu's fingers itched with the need to soothe the wrinkles. She waggled her head. "Only a little. Besides, technically, he's not my boyfriend, and I didn't really invite him. He invited himself."

"That's the first I've heard of this." Stu leaned towards Poppy. Sure, he might have begged her to ask him along today, but he considered himself her boyfriend, lover, whatever you want to call it.

"Maybe you two need to have a little talk." Christo grinned, his smile stretching from ear to ear. "Good luck, Stu." Christo walked off towards the group huddled around the BBQ, although to call it that was something of an understatement, given the size of the lamb roasting on a spit. There was enough food there to feed a hundred people.

"You invited me. Are you having second thoughts?" Stu must have portrayed more confidence than he felt inside as she tilted her head to the side and considered him.

"How old are you?" Poppy's question made him frown.

"Why?"

"They—" She flicked her head towards the house. "—All think you are too old for me. And since I don't know your age…"

He leaned in close to her, whispering in her ear. "You know my hair is fake, right?"

She barked out a laugh and thumped him on the chest.

"I turned thirty last month. I was only twenty eight when I first met you, and I desperately needed a way to look older. Clients thought I was too baby-faced to do business with."

"And now my family think you are, like, forty five and Mama is worried that I have daddy issues." Poppy bit her bottom lip.

"Forty-five! You should be proud. Your work creates exactly the impression I wanted." He paused as she smiled up at him, a light pink flush on her cheeks, but the little frown between her eyebrows didn't go away. "Something else is bothering you."

"Goddamn it, Stu. Does my face give away all my thoughts?" She turned away from him to stare at the large olive tree in the bottom of the backyard.

"I've spent two years watching you closely as you work. I'd like to think I can read your expressions quite well."

"You know that sounds quite creepy." Poppy grinned at him, shaking her head slightly.

"Yeah, that's me. Creepy as all hell. No wonder your brother thinks he needs to put the hard word on me." Stu tucked an errant strand of bright blue hair behind her ear, enjoying the little tingles on his fingertips as he touched her skin.

"It's nothing much."

"You are annoyed that Christo called me your boyfriend." Stu guessed at the truth.

"Yes. It implies too much. You are a fuck buddy, that's all."

Stu swallowed back an irritated gasp, his nostrils flaring. "How many other fuck buddies have you invited to a family party?"

Poppy closed her eyes. "Only you."

"I rather think that warrants giving me a more encompassing label." Stu instinctively knew this wasn't the time to push her, to ask her to do this for the long term. He took a deep breath.

"It's only been two days, Stu. Two intense days. Far too short for labels." Poppy smoothed out her shirt, as Stu realised her truth. He'd been interested in Poppy for two years. This was all new for her. He'd have to be cautious, to give her the time she needed to adjust to his view of them.

13

Poppy watched Stu charm all her relatives as everyone ate a late lunch and toasted Greece with cries of Oxi Oxi and plenty of ouzo. Even mean old Aunt Marie smiled at him as he regaled stories and encouraged her family to talk about themselves, and about her. Poppy realised she enjoyed his company, and the relaxed way he fitted into her clan added to a growing sense of wonder about him. She'd spent so long thinking about him as a hot client, someone whose hair she cut, but whose world she knew nothing about. And now, he just belonged. In only two days, he'd managed to effectively place himself in her life until she could barely imagine her life without him. What utter madness. If she wasn't careful this would be Jean-Phillipe and his fake promises all over again.

"How did you meet Stu?" Aunt Christina's comment broke into Poppy's thoughts.

"At work." Meaning that she cut his hair, and without

Stu taking charge of the situation and asking her out for a drink, that's all she would have ever had.

"Poppy is very talented. You should all be proud of her." Stu slid his arm around her waist as he interrupted the conversation. Poppy flinched, the muscles in her shoulder tightening.

"Did you just say you met at work?" Aunt Christina's gaze switched between the two of them.

"I cut his hair." Poppy clarified. Seriously, they all knew she worked at Spiro's, because some of them had been so cut up about her inheriting the business. She bit back the sarcastic, *what other work might it be?*

"And she does a marvellous job."

"Later, Stu. We don't need to discuss that now."

"Hold on. If you cut his hair, and you said you met at work, well, I'm a little confused." Aunt Christina raised one eyebrow.

Stu smiled, his wolf on the prowl smile making Poppy's chest glow with warmth. "Let me tell you a little story. One sunny day, I was walking along the street in Surry Hills, when I spied a barber's shop. One of those typical old school shops, so ancient it was almost retro-cool. A blackboard sat outside on the path, and on it were written the words "Champion Colourist". I had no idea what that meant. The understated lack of marketing for a statement which should be shouted out loud tugged at my curiosity, so I went inside to discover more."

"You didn't tell me that." Poppy had assumed that he'd entered her shop because she was a champion colourist, and he wanted a highly technical colour. He winked at her, and she clamped her lips shut before she blurted out his secret.

"I entered the shop, with one question on my mind. Why would a champion hide?"

"Stop right there. My sign has never said 'champion colourist', it says 'specialist in colour treatments'."

Stu chuckled. "You can't ruin my story with facts. Never mind the sign, the point of my tale is—"

"Yes?" Poppy couldn't help herself. What was Stu's point with this story? And why did Aunt Christina keep glancing at them both with an inane grin on her face?

"The moment I stepped inside the shop, Spiros, I knew my life had changed forever. Standing in the middle of the floor was the most beautiful woman I'd ever seen, with bright red hair. A flame for a moth like me." Stu's hand tightened on her waist, as her knees softened with every word. He thought she was beautiful that day?

"Bright red hair?" Aunt Christina queried.

"Two years ago, I had vivid garnet hair in a 1920s bob cut."

"It shone like a flaming halo around your head, and I couldn't look away." Stu had Aunt Christina convinced. Poppy wanted to roll her eyes and ask him why it took him two years to find the time to ask her out, except if she resorted to snark, she'd never hear the end of this story.

"What a beautiful, romantic story." Aunt Christina sighed, clutching her hands to her substantial bosom. The whole family had been blessed with the same shape, and no matter how much Poppy swam or ran or did stupidly annoying gym work, her heart stayed fit, and her body stayed plump. She'd long ago come to terms with her shape. It was what is was, and while her body wasn't fashionable, she enjoyed the way she drew Stu's attention as he happily told her family she was beautiful. Poppy shook her head.

"Why shake your head, Calliope? This man, he understands romance. You are a lucky girl."

"No, Christina, I am a lucky man to have Poppy in my life." Stu dragged his fingers up her spine, then traced small circles on the back of Poppy's neck, under the nape of her hair, and all she could imagine was the short black hairs on the backs of his hand brushing past the bright long strands of her hair.

"Come along Stu, enough charming my aunties, come and talk to Papa." Poppy stepped away from the spell he weaved, hoping that her father's brand of common sense would help her stay grounded.

"So lovely to meet you Stu. Are you sure you aren't Greek?"

He shrugged. "Not on my mother's side. It has been a delight to talk to you, Christina. Another time." He must have rushed to walk beside her because he appeared at her side, and as soon as they were a few paces away from Christina, Stu whispered. "The Greeks don't want to be claiming my father." The hard undertone in his voice made Poppy tilt her head with curiosity.

"Why not?"

"I'll tell you later. Now isn't the time for terrible tales. I'd rather talk to your father without the distraction of mine."

"Sure. Makes sense." Poppy swallowed away the hint of bile that rose at his dismissal. She wanted to know his story. Was he just fobbing her off? Or was he right?

"I will tell you later. I want to be open with you. It's important to me."

"Okay."

Hours later, full of conversation, cake, and with a happy buzz of too much alcohol, Poppy fell into a cab with Stu.

"My place?"

"Yeah." Poppy rested her head back on the seat. The whole afternoon hadn't been a disaster, and Stu had seemed to fit into the huge Karahalios clan easily.

"Are you alright?"

"I'm fine. I should be asking you the same question. You've been quiet. Well, quieter than usual since Aunt Christina mentioned your heritage."

"Do you think anyone else noticed?"

"No. Don't worry about it." Poppy reassured him. Was he so obsessed with appearances that he stressed about whether a group of people he'd only met once approved of him?

"Alright. I'm good. I'm good."

"Are you?"

Stu let out a shaky long breath. One that Poppy only noticed, because he was leaning against her. The sickly sweet liquorice of Ouzo filled her nostrils.

"Yeah, I'm good. Have I told you how fucking lucky you are to have a loving family?"

"Stu, how much Ouzo did they make you drink? You'll be in Ouzo world soon."

"Ouzo world?"

"It's a happy cartoon world where everything is amazing."

"Everything is amazing. Your family is the best. I think I love them."

Poppy shook her head, unable to prevent a grin breaking out at his lavish comment. "Settle down, Stu. That's just the Ouzo talking."

"Maybe a little, but you must know how awesome your family is. I'm so goddamned jealous."

"We are an ordinary family, I mean, there are a lot of us which is probably a bit unusual, but we are all just ordinary people." Poppy stroked his arm, the muscles perfectly shaped under her fingertips.

"You have love for each other. Support. I mean, my mum is totally amazing. She brought me up all on her own, and fuck, I was a shit as a teenager. She did an amazing job to hold everything together."

"Stu, are you saying it's just you and your mum?" Poppy couldn't imagine a world without her busy-body aunts, and her multitude of cousins. Imagine having no cousins to turn to when a parent annoyed you, or no one to call when something went wrong. Friends only went so far. She could always trust family to help her out, even if it came at the cost of their opinions on what she needed to do to resolve whatever problem she'd asked about.

"Your aunt asked if I was Greek…"

"Yeah, and you muttered something about not wanting to claim your father. Can you tell me about him?" Poppy figured she may as well ask while he was drunk. He'd called his mum amazing twice in one sentence, and he loved talking. Surely, she could get him to talk about tricky subjects while he was happily inebriated.

"There isn't much to tell. Mum won't talk about. He's not listed on my birth certificate. I've always assumed she'd been raped because she refuses to discuss it. That's why I'll never force myself on anyone. I won't be the dickhead who doesn't respect people's boundaries." Stu sat up straight, his gaze glued to the seat in front of him.

Poppy placed her hand gently on his thigh. She hadn't expected that impassioned spray. She blinked a few times. "Stu, you are the most courteous lover I've ever had. Stop worrying about it. You aren't him. You couldn't possibly be." More than simply courteous, Poppy loved and admired the way he always put her needs at the forefront.

"Why do you say that? How can you be so certain that I don't share elements with him?"

"Science."

"What? That's not what I thought you'd say."

"I read a lot when the salon is quiet. And I read that a baby does over two thirds of its brain development after it is born. If your father left the scene when you were only a few cells old, he has no influence on you."

"Apart from genetics."

Poppy shrugged. "So you might look like him. I believe that all people are born nice, and they learn to be horrible, if that's what life teaches them. Without him in your life, you couldn't learn to be like him. He doesn't influence your choices."

"Thank you. Did I tell you your family is amazing?"

"You sure did." Poppy nodded and laughed, warmed all the way through by his joy at her family. She kissed his cheek. "It's sweet of you to say that."

"I've always wanted—" Stu slammed his lips shut and stared out the window.

"A big family?" Poppy guessed.

"How did you guess?"

"Easy. People always want what they don't have. And you already have everything else. Career, money, great looks, confidence. Family is all that is missing."

"Right. I guess that's pretty transparent then." Stu turned towards her, his gaze slightly dazed. Was that the Ouzo, or the topic?

"Hey, it's fine. Everyone has something they don't have that they want."

"But you already have family, a gorgeous personality and mouth watering looks. What more could you want?"

"A successful business. Money and a career." Between Jean-Phillipe smashing her confidence, and the long fight to believe in herself again, combined with the drag of running Spiro's, her dreams had taken a backburner to the frustrations of reality.

"I can make Spiro's amazing if you'll let me work some marketing magic." His state of inebriation hadn't dimmed his confidence at all, unlike the doubt she harboured.

"Can you now?" Poppy wished her heart didn't speed up in hope. Any changes she made would create more fuss than Stu's appearance at Oxi Day today. She could already hear the outcries over Pappous' legacy, mostly because she'd heard it a million times before.

"Yeah. Because it has the one thing that a good business needs."

"What's that, Stu?" Poppy tried to keep the excitement out of her voice, tried to stay cautious.

"You."

"I'm what a good business needs? If that was true, I'd be rolling in cash already. Go to sleep, Stu, and wake up when the ouzo has worn off."

"No, I mean it. A good business needs someone with passion to drive it forward. You have that. You just need a few tools to get you there."

"And you have those tools?"

"Yeah. Yeah, I do." The cab pulled up outside Stu's townhouse in Surry Hills. For only the second time in her life, Poppy tumbled out of a car with Stu towards this house. In only a few short days, so much had changed. Stu walked without a stumble, without any sway in his steps, nothing to give away his rambling talk in the car. Poppy followed him, amazed that this confident executive in control of his life believed in her, when she thought she was the only person who believed in her. Stu turned to her, one hand on the front door key, one hand held outstretched for her.

"Front steps, hallway, or my bed."

She giggled, overcome by memories of her first visit to

this house. "I don't think … we should … give the driver a show." She managed to get the sentence out between panted breaths. No amount of ouzo would convince her to have sex on the front doorstep.

"Bed, then?" Stu rattled the key in the lock, as she nodded, then they both stumbled inside. Poppy didn't know who kissed first, but soon they were lip-locked, scrambling down the hallway in a race for Stu's bedroom. Kisses, laughter, and limbs all in a flurry. Poppy pushed past him and ran up the stairs.

"Shall I chase you?"

"Yes. Chase me. Fling me on the bed. Have your wonderful way with me."

The ring of fire in his eyes burned brighter, as his eyes darkened before her face. "I love the way you think." He tumbled her to the bed. Clothes flew. Skin torched each other. And they raced together, heart beats in time, to a clumsy, inelegant, perfectly wonderful, end-of-party release.

"Holy Zeus, you are good." Words pretty much failed Poppy as she lay collapsed, sated on his high thread count sheets. The luxury of his sheets only made the frantic experience more amazing, to use Stu's favourite drunken word.

"Good, you mean amazing." Stu slurred a little and it made the declaration sound sweeter.

Poppy clamped her hand over her mouth as a giggle threatened to erupt.

"Hell, we nearly set the sheets on fire. Anymore and I'll have to keep a fire extinguisher in my bedroom." He nuzzled against her neck.

"Could you say anything more Stu-like?" Poppy's giggle burst out. She realised she'd grown used to his over the top phrasing, it made her smile instead of wonder if he really meant it.

14

Somewhere in the post Oxi Day party week, Poppy had fallen into a routine with Stu. Her routine hadn't changed much, she still spent all day doing boring haircuts so she could pay Levi and all her other expenses. She still went home every evening on the train to hang out with Dread as she did the accounts. But now she answered the phone every lunch time.

"Yes, Stu, I've eaten properly."

And she didn't eat dinner alone. He dropped by every night, seemingly happy to sit beside her on the couch with his laptop. Poppy smiled. She bounced through each day knowing that she'd get great sex at the end of the day with her hot boyfriend. Her life seemed blissfully surreal and when her phone rang, she answered with lightness in her heart.

"Mama." Poppy answered the phone as she rode the train home one evening.

"I need to talk to you about the salon. Several people in

the family have been worried since meeting your Stu…" Mama didn't pause. Poppy's thoughts drifted away at those fateful words 'your Stu'. Yes, he did seem to be occupying that role in her life. After a frantic start, he'd settled into her life. No longer was it her, Dread, and the salon. Stu joined in too.

"Are you listening to me?"

"Huh, I'm sorry, Mama, what did you say?"

"Damn it, girl. Pay attention. People are worried about the salon. It's our heritage, and some people think—"

"Yes, some people, particularly Aunt Maria, think the expensive real estate should have gone to her son, not to me. But I was the one who turned up every day to run the business for Pappou. I'm the one who worked for this. Shouldn't I get a say in the next phase of the business?" Poppy bunched her fists in her shirt.

"Where is that coming from? Poppy, you've always been so quiet and compliant."

Poppy dragged in a deep breath and tried not to grind her teeth. Compliant. Bullshit. "I know what people say about me. You know some of the family is jealous."

"All the more reason to stop Stu from trampling all over the family business. You can't let a stranger arrange your life."

"What nonsense have you been listening too?" Poppy frowned, her brain racing at the implications.

"Just a few of us. We all met him. He's charming and powerful. We are all worried that he's too much for you."

Right. Nice of Mama to believe she couldn't attract someone like Stu. Thanks for the support. Poppy swallowed back the snarky thoughts. Stu liked her, as apparently incredible as that seemed to others. "Mama. Stu is…"

"He's a confident executive who will throw you away when he finds a better option. Men like that don't marry girls like you."

"Who said anything about marriage?" Poppy tried to ignore the way Mama zeroed in on her doubts. Her stomach churned and she pressed one hand against it.

"Calliope, we just want you to be happy."

"I am happy."

"Just remember that we are all family, and we matter more than some bloke." Mama's final statement was delivered with a command. Poppy nodded softly as the disconnection beep sounded in her ear.

T he station took way too long to arrive, but eventually Poppy stepped off the train, stormed home, and flung open her door. She paced inside, threw her bag on the couch and marched to the fridge. She opened a bottle of cheap champagne and poured herself a glass. She sat, cross-legged on the couch, and Dread leapt into her lap.

"Ahh, kitty, what am I to do? Marie is in Mama's ear about the salon. Damn it, just because she married Pappous' oldest son doesn't mean she should have his entire estate." Poppy stroked Dread's fur, each motion soothing her after such a jarring conversation. The front door creaked open. "Fucking patriarchy."

"What's the celebration?" Stu strode into her apartment, his blue eyes dancing. Poppy shook her head.

"No celebration. Mama just called."

"And?" Stu sat beside her, pressing a kiss to her cheek.

Poppy sighed. "I'd better give you some background before I launch into this. Pappou—"

"The famous Spiro?"

"Yeah." Poppy rolled her eyes at Stu's enthusiasm. "He had four children, Spiro, Dimitris, Nick, and Mama. Spiro married Aunt Maria who you met at Oxi Day."

"Spiro the older, or Spiro the son?"

"The son."

"Ahh, I see the problem. Maria believes she should have all the important parts of the estate and is annoyed that you got the Surry Hills property."

Poppy let out a long sigh. Not only had Stu charmed her family, but he also instinctively understood all the little politics. "In a nutshell, yes. And she's always in Mama's ear about preserving Pappous' legacy and doing the right thing by him."

Stu rubbed his temple. "Can I ask you a question?"

"Of course."

"Setting aside family loyalty, what is actually stopping you doing what you want? Do you owe money to one of the family?"

"Stu, I can't set aside family loyalty. It's not about what Maria says, it's simply because I loved Pappous. I worked closely with him for years as he slowly got old and his hands turned arthritic. I know how he felt about the salon, and I preserve it for him. The challenge isn't so much Maria and Mama, although their opinions are hard to ignore, it's about balancing out my goals and my memories."

"What if we can find a way to do both?"

Poppy shut her eyes and tried to ignore the way her heart leapt in hope. She daren't answer.

Stu filled the space with the most important question of all. "And what would Pappous want you to do?"

"He wasn't much for big dreams. He'd had a tough life, being a teenager in Greece during the war while the country was ravaged by occupied forces tends to make your dreams small. He only wanted safety, security, nothing flashy. A quiet business to work in every day that provides good, simple service, and a regular income for his family."

"Those are excellent goals."

Poppy sat up straighter and stared at Stu. "What aren't you saying?"

"His goals make sense for him, and the time he grew up, for his era. They don't make sense for someone with your talents. And they don't make sense for our modern world. You should take a risk on your brilliance."

"You are presuming a lot of brilliance on my part." Her heart continued to gallop.

"Based on my experience. Remember when I first entered the salon and told you what I wanted. And you said I must consider how to make the transition look natural. You gave me two options; to go grey slowly over the course of several months, or to go grey straightaway, but be prepared to tell people I'd been dying out the grey."

"You chose the latter. How did that work out for you?"

"Easy. It helps having jet black hair, people think the colour is already unreal. Vince, the hardest person in the world to convince, said that it was a good look leaving the grey in place. Made me look older, more experienced."

Poppy gulped her champagne and changed the subject. "There is some beer in the fridge if you want something." She had no response for his enthusiasm. It was one thing for her to believe in herself and her talent, quite another for him to do the same. Stu bounced off the couch, and she twisted to watch him. Dread poked his talons into her jeans, a little warning that he didn't want her to move. She huffed at him and stroked his fur. Dread relaxed back into his purring snooze.

"Do you mind if I make some notes?" Stu sank onto the couch next to her.

"Yeah, I guess." Poppy couldn't quite line up his enthusiasm with the remnants of Mama's words still rattling around her brain. She didn't want to disappoint anyone. Why did that need result in her disappointment with herself?

Stu reached up and stroked her cheek. "Poppy, you have passion and talent. Passion is a fragile thing, a kind of magic that can't be taught. It makes people into great leaders, or wonderful artists. I don't want to see your loyalty to your family crush that passion out of you. I have the skills to grow your passion for hair into reality. Let's make the world know about your talent."

Poppy could only stare, open mouthed at Stu. How had she, a plain, plump hairdresser that no one saw, been seen by someone like Stu? He embodied success, while she stumbled from day to day. He was fashionably hot. Her body shape hadn't been trendy for hundreds of years. He had supreme confidence. She swayed between doubt and hopeful arrogance several times during each day. His involvement with her made no sense, and she couldn't shake Mama's opinion that Stu was slumming it with her. A temporary arrangement that he'd toss away like a piece of crumpled paper when he was done with chasing variety. Maybe he'd chase another misfit who didn't belong in his corporate world. She wanted to believe him. Oh boy, did she ever. Why did he have to be so unbelievable?

Stu thumbed open his phone. "Spiro's has been around since when?"

"1949."

"Excellent. Nostalgia is a real trend at the moment, it's the core of the hipster movement, you know retro-cool."

"You mentioned that about the salon once before." Poppy stared at Stu, unable to look away as he concentrated on her business. Hers. There was something so hot, so elemental about watching him focus his energy on her. Worry flew away, replaced with a wet heat welling between her legs. She went to clench her thighs together, but Dread reminded her of his presence with another lazy swipe of his paw.

"Retro-cool. That's the look we are going to run with. Let's get some photos of Spiro for the walls, update the signage to reflect that. It'll be cheap to throw some photos on social media, maybe offer a few free cuts to beautiful young people in return for promotional photos. We'll get people talking."

Poppy's eyes widened. Could it be as easy as he said?

"The only cost will be the exterior. We'll have to do a redesign to make it more welcoming."

"What about my current clients?"

"Keep them." Stu shrugged as if it was so easy.

"Um…"

"No, seriously, we aren't going to do anything crazy like massively lift prices for a simple cut. Your core business will stay the same. All we are doing is a makeover on the front with a retro-cool funky look, and to get people talking about you. Do you blog?"

"No. When would I have time?" Poppy shrugged.

"What about Levi? Can he write? It'd be great if you could do a fashion photo type of blog for some of the fancier cuts and colours. Actually, it wouldn't need to have loads of words; let the photos do the talking. I'll set it up and it won't take much to maintain it."

"You have all the answers, don't you?" Poppy wanted to sound cynical, except he gave her a look of confident belief in her. There was a buzz in her ears and suddenly a grin burst across her face. It really was possible.

"And for the longer term, when you have a bit more cash, you can put a telly in the front window, and stream photos of people's hair that you've done." Stu waved his hands as he spoke, his whole body energised. Poppy stopped resisting. She picked up Dread and lay him on the couch in his own spot. Twisting back towards Stu, she cradled his face in her hands and kissed him.

"Brilliant. When can we start?"

"You like it?"

"Stu, you had me sold when you mentioned putting up heritage style photos of Pappous. He would love that, especially if we throw in some of the village in Greece, and early Surry Hills… You know how it looked when he first arrived here."

"I told you I was good." Stu grinned smugly.

Poppy shook her head. "Stop talking Stu and kiss me."

Magic words, those. Kissing Poppy had quickly become one of his favourite things. He didn't really understand why she let her family hold her back from success. He'd never let his less than perfect upbringing hold him back. At the first touch of her lips against his, desire roared to life. Poppy moaned against his mouth. Fuck, he loved the way she responded to him. Every single time. He cradled one of her gorgeous full breasts, cupping the weight. Perfection. He pinched her nipple and she gasped. Her tongue pushed inside his mouth, sweet popping candy tastes exploding on his tongue.

"Poppy. I want to fuck your breasts."

Her eyes popped wide open. "How?" Not maybe. His body hummed with desire as she asked the perfect question.

"Strip."

"Sure." Her snarky answer only made him harder. Fuck. Magic Poppy and her mouthy words. She threaded her hands into his hair, making no effort to do as she was told, only deepening their kiss. He pulled back, grabbed her shirt in his fists and ripped it up towards her neck. A hiss from Dread reminded him they weren't alone.

"Damned cat."

Poppy laughed. "If you feed him, he'll stay in the kitchen."

Stu picked up Dread and carried him to the kitchen. He quickly grabbed some cat biscuits for the fierce one-eyed creature and plopped him gently on the floor.

"Are you nude yet?" Stu had spent enough time with Poppy to know when she was ready to play a power game with him.

"Make me." Her eyes flashed and his chest swelled with pride. Anticipation. Yeah, she knew. He leaned over her, one hand on the back of the couch for balance. He stroked the other hand up her jeans, from her knee to her waistband. Only a tremble of her thighs gave away her arousal. Her gaze stayed glued to his. He hooked his finger under her waistband, flicked open her jeans.

"I bet you are wet for me."

"Find out." She licked her bottom lip, and shifted on the couch slightly, making her breasts wobble. His dick pressed insistent against his pants. He grabbed her shirt and ripped. Fabric tore, buttons popped off, and Poppy's mouth dropped open in shock.

"Stu!"

"I can buy you another shirt." Desire roared in his ears. Holy fuck. Her breasts, covered in black lace, were everything. He lowered himself over her, his hips grinding against hers, freeing up both his hands. She reached out for his shirt, tugging it out of his waistband.

"No." He took her hands and held them above her head. Her eyes widened again as he lowered his mouth to her throat. Her skin tasted of Poppy, sweet, sultry, and all his. With one finger, he traced the edge of her bra, enjoying the way gooseflesh pebbled on her skin. He pushed her bra down, releasing her breast to him. All the beautiful round flesh. His. He sucked her dark nipple into his mouth, the hard bud on his tongue. Poppy moaned, screamed, making all the breathy sex sounds as he used his mouth on her.

"Stu." Yes, Poppy. He wanted her to call his name, beg for release. She wriggled underneath him, and pulled her hands away from his grasp, then slipped them behind her back. Her bra pinged loose, and she collapsed back, dragging her hands up his arms. He flung the bra aside and buried his head between her breasts. Her breathy pants continued as he rasped her skin with his stubble, deliberately roughing her soft skin.

"Poppy." He licked the sore spots he'd made, soothing them.

"Yes?" Poppy's hands slid down his back, loose and relaxed. He flicked her nipples, and her fingers clung deep into his spine.

"Come now." He sucked her nipple again, smiling against her breast as she obeyed him. Her head fell back as she cried out, her eyes shut. He rose above her with his knees either side of her hips, and she lifted her hips as his weight left her. With his hand, he pressed down on her stomach to keep her in place.

"Stu. Please."

"You want more?"

"Fuck yes." That was his Poppy; dirty when she begged him and he fucking adored it. She grabbed his hand and pushed it down. He slid a finger under her panties, grazing her curls as he used his palm to prevent her from bucking.

"More." She demanded.

"No."

"What!" Poppy half sat up, her eyes flying open in aroused outrage. "Why not?"

"Me first." His dick swelled at her need for him, the way her full lips were reddened by his kiss, the way his stubble had marked her skin. Mostly, at the way she required his fingers inside her. He slid closer to her clit, teasing.

"Yes. Stu. Like that." His name on her lips almost ending his control. He wanted to give her everything she asked for.

"This will be better." He managed to croak out the words. And fuck, she hadn't even touched his dick yet. "Take off my pants. Hold me."

Poppy tilted her head to the side, considering. She sucked her bottom lip into her mouth, slowly releasing it as she stared at the way his cock strained at his pants. After the world's longest pause, she undid his pants, and dragged them over his hips. His cock stood to attention. Ready. Poppy brushed her thumb across the top, making a circle with the bead of pre-come.

"Yes. Hold me tight."

"And you'll reward me."

"If you obey." He saw the war in her eyes. The battle of desire over rebellion. Need won, obviously, as her hand gripped him tight, sliding up and down his length. He dragged in a tight breath as her perfect hand urged him on. Stu pushed his fingers into her slick, wet opening, immediately rewarded with Poppy's breathless moans. Time slowed as she clenched around his fingers, crying out. Her own hand tight on his cock. He lowered himself over her, knees against her waist and his hand stretched behind him, until his cock nestled between her breasts. It was a bit awkward, but he didn't care.

"Hold your breasts. Tight over me." Stu commanded, although his voice came out all breathy. His legs pressed into the couch for balanced with one hand beside Poppy's head for stability and the other stretched down between her legs to stroke Poppy's clit. The bundle of nerves hardened, as Poppy panted rapidly in time with his own aching lungs. Her little cries grew stronger, and she complied with his command without argument.

"Yes, that's it." The soft, plush flesh of her breasts pushed against his cock. He fucked her breasts, matching each thrust with a thrust of his fingers into Poppy. Thrusting until they both cried out. Stu shouted her name to the world as she tightened around his fingers. He came hard, his seed splashing over Poppy's neck. Painting her with a necklace of his desire. It was everything in one picture. The most glorious painting of his own creation. He wanted to cherish this moment forever. He let out a shaky breath as her eyes flickered slowly open, her beautiful brown eyes sated and sleepy. Perfection.

15

———

Poppy flicked her hair as she used the rideshare car's mirrors to assess her new colour. The bright red flashed underneath the black overtones. Levi's skill had improved nicely, and the new cut and colour he'd done today had come up a treat. The black and red would match the black silk dress she'd purchased for tonight's fancy dinner. The dress flowed over her body, wrapped around her waist to highlight her breasts, along with the red sash clinched around her waist. She'd combined the dress with a red beaded necklace and red pumps. The choice of nude lipstick had been a good one; more red would have been too over the top. Would Stu like it? She hoped so. She could barely believe that he'd asked her to this dinner. The Annual Australian Advertising Awards. What was it about a big public appearance that made their relationship seem real? She breathed in and out. And what did it say about her that she didn't care what the world thought of her? Only what

Stu thought. He'd demonstrated his desire for her in so many ways, she had no room for doubt.

Stu: How's things?

Poppy: Pulling into your street now. Poppy hit send, and muttered. "As planned. Don't stress. I'll be on time."

Stu: Excellent. Poppy thanked the driver as she exited the car.

"Hey, gorgeous." Stu stood on the front doorstep, his handsome strong body outfitted in a perfect black suit with a navy tie. As she walked towards him, his smile grew, and the subtle embroidered paisley pattern of his tie made his eyes bluer in the sharp late spring evening light. The weather had already begun its march into summer with its hot nights and hotter days.

"You're looking quite fine too." A strong rush of ownership buzzed in Poppy's veins. She would be the one on Stu's arm tonight. He'd picked her.

"Maybe we should give the dinner a miss…" Stu winked.

Poppy shook her head. "Nah. Not after all this effort to get ready." She waved her hand in the direction of her head and smiled when Stu's lips parted.

"You changed your hair."

"It's hardly a subtle change, Stu. Surely, you noticed?"

He shifted his shoulders. "I was too busy staring at your other … um, assets."

"You mean, my boobs." Poppy leaned against his arm and whispered into his ear. Deliberately, she pressed her breasts against him. Her nipples pebbled as a muscle tightened in his jaw.

"Are you trying to keep me at home?" Gravel filled Stu's voice.

Poppy laughed. "If you'd prefer."

Stu swallowed, his throat moving before he ran his hand through his hair. "Damn it, I really have to be there tonight."

"There is always afterwards." Poppy started to laugh, except the sound was absorbed by Stu's kiss.

Three hours later, and all the awards had been given out and applauded. A statuette stood proud on their table, and Stu beamed as streams of people walked past their table to congratulate him. Poppy knew she'd had too much champagne, as a heady pride infused her smile.

"Cleveland." A sharpness in Vince's voice made her head flick up. A tall, grey haired white man stood by their table. Stu and Vince stood up, and Poppy wondered if she should too. Stu gave Vince a warning look, and Vince nodded then walked away from their group.

"Poppy, I'd like you to meet Mr Cleveland." Stu spoke as though none of those odd glances had happened, with only politeness in his tone.

"Hi." Poppy leaped to her feet, stuck out her hand towards the old guy and he shook it with two hands. The corner of Stu's eye twitched.

"And this is Mr Cleveland's daughter, Jamie." Stu glanced at the tall blonde standing beside him, then stared at Poppy's hand as she tugged it free from Mr Cleveland's grasp. Poppy shook out her fingers, trying not to wipe the clamminess down her dress. Jamie flicked her hair back, and Poppy couldn't help assessing the sway in her cut. Her hair was flawless.

"Nice to see you, Cooper. Congratulations on the award. Where did your boss get to?" Cleveland looked around the room, then left to chase his target. Poppy hoped Vince knew how to deal with the slightly slimy Cleveland.

"Stu, it's been so long since we caught up." Jamie's gaze roamed with a lack of subtlety and decency over Stu's body.

"I see you are a member of the Stu Arse Appreciation Society too." Oh fuck, Poppy squeezed her eyes shut. She really had had too much of that incredibly tasty champagne. She'd meant to ask Jamie who did her hair, not blurt out the most awkward thing in the history of the world. Ever. Fortunately her comment had been timed with the band starting up. Poppy prayed no one had heard her.

"Excuse me?" Stu asked. Did that mean he hadn't heard her properly? Jamie's eyes narrowed in speculation. She definitely had heard her Freudian slip. Blast.

"I said—" Poppy cleared her throat, "I like your hair, Jamie. Where did you get it done?"

Stu squinted. Jamie smiled, although it didn't reach her eyes.

"Jean-Phillipe's Grand Salon. He is worth every cent."

Poppy felt her face go white, and she swallowed. "Yes, Jean-Phillipe is one of the best."

"You know him?" Stu asked. Poppy could only nod.

"I don't mean to be rude, but you don't look like you could afford Jean-Phillipe. Unless Stu is paying, of course."

"It's not rude." Even though it was totally rude and

intended to sting. Poppy's fists clenched at her sides. "I did my initial training with Jean-Phillipe, before we didn't see eye to eye on certain creative aspects." She dragged in a deep breath. Jean-Phillipe's version of creativity included bedding as many of his apprentices as he could, preferably at the same time. "I finished my apprenticeship with Nora Fields, who now resides in Hollywood. She won an Oscar for design last year."

"You are a hairdresser?" Jamie asked.

"That's amazing." Stu spoke at the same time as Jamie.

Poppy smiled ruefully. "Yes. And what is it you do, Jamie?"

"I'm a society blogger." Jamie made her statement with pride. Poppy's confusion must have shown on her face.

Stu nodded once. "Jamie has over 100,000 followers."

"My blog does super well because I go to all the best parties. Everyone who is anyone knows they have to invite me."

"Well, lovely to meet you Jamie. I need to go and powder my nose." Poppy wrinkled her nose at Stu, as she pulled out a silly old-fashioned euphemism. She didn't really need to go to the toilet, she just needed some breathing space from this conversation. She didn't need listen to Jamie, model thin with an apparently important father, as she disparaged her career choice. Society blogger; what on earth did that mean?

"I'll come with you." Jamie smiled, again with her calculating grimace. A stray thought made Poppy grin. If Jamie actually smiled properly, she'd be gorgeous with her plump lips and favourable genetics. Oh, shit. Poppy gritted her teeth to acknowledge the streak of jealously that flared up. She swallowed and started walking through the room.

"I bet this is all very glamourous for you." Jamie sneered. Poppy pretended she didn't hear over the band who pounded out old glam rock classics while everyone in the room ignored the music to talk to each other.

"I said, I bet this…"

"I heard what you said." Poppy narrowed her eyes as she considered Jamie. "I take it you aren't accompanying me to the toilet for polite company." The soundproofing in this building was impressive, as the sound of the band and all that rapid fire conversation from hundreds of people faded away as soon as they stepped into the hallway leading to the toilets.

"Oh, so you do have some social understanding, then." Jamie's hips swayed under her impossibly tight dress as she stepped in front of Poppy. Poppy waited. Everything about this woman screamed confrontation, and Poppy almost grinned. At least this wasn't boring. Unlike the three hours of self-congratulation she'd listened to as the awards were given out.

"You don't belong here."

"In the hallway with you?" Poppy deliberately baited her. She wasn't going to give any hint that she'd had the exact same thought only a few minutes ago.

"No. You know what I mean."

"Perhaps you might like to expand…"

"I don't know what Stu sees in you. He's just using you to get back at me."

"Is that so?" Poppy huffed out a hard laugh. Was Jamie

an ex-girlfriend? The hallway confrontation suddenly became a lot more interesting.

"Yes. He doesn't want you. A nobody. He needs me."

"A somebody?" Poppy couldn't help asking the obvious question. Jamie had a rather inflated view of herself; probably all those society parties and all that hanging out with Sydney's important people.

"Yes. Stu is going to be one of the greats of the advertising world. He needs someone who understands how this game works."

"And it upsets you that he doesn't see the world the same way you do?"

"Yes! One little mistake and he won't talk to me. And now he flaunts you. Just because you look like his favourite painting. He's a fool." Jamie sniffed and flicked her head. Poppy pressed her lips together to prevent her mouth dropping open. Where should she start in processing that spray of information? Jamie knew Stu's favourite painting? Was that the one he'd mentioned once before? Something about Magdalene? Poppy realised Jamie was waiting for a response.

"Shouldn't you pay for your mistakes? The rest of us have to."

"It's about the bigger picture. Anyone who knows Vince knows the idea that I would cheat on Stu with Vince is ridiculous." Jamie put her hands on her hips in an indignant pose, as Poppy swallowed back a splutter of a laugh.

"Hold on. Are you saying Stu dumped you when he found you kissing his boss?"

If Jamie's eyes held bullets, Poppy would have been dead

many times over from the glare. Poppy didn't try to hold back her laughter anymore.

"Oh that's gold. And you think confronting me will help your case? I'll tell you one thing."

"Yeah?"

"You are right. I don't belong here." Poppy paused as a sly smile began on Jamie's full lips. "But I know one thing. Stu appreciates loyalty, and no matter how mean you are to me, it won't change the fact that you tried to use Stu as a stepping stone to Vince."

Jamie gasped. She slapped Poppy across the face. Sharp pain flooded her cheek, reverberating in her teeth.

"How dare you talk about Vince like that? It was nothing like that."

Poppy rubbed her face. "How dare I what?"

"Vince is my friend. I've never kissed him."

"Right, because why bother with the 2IC when you could have the billionaire boss?" Poppy asked. "Unless—" Poppy drew out that word as logic prevailed. "Vince rejected you."

"He didn't reject me. He… It's not what you think. Stu, obviously…" Jamie gave Poppy a snide once-over with her gaze, "has no standards. And since he's a shareholder in Kapow too—"

Poppy rubbed her cheek and tried not to buckle under the implication about Stu's standards. Because hell, if he'd slept with Jamie, his standards were definitely questionable. And what did that say about Poppy? She cut in over Jamie's spray. "—And you say I don't belong here. You only care about the money."

"You wouldn't know what it's like." Jamie rubbed her hands together, in a gesture that would look like guilt on anyone else. She pushed away her concern. Jamie didn't get to be guilty for lashing out at her.

"To be a gold-digger?" Poppy wasn't sure who was being more audacious; her or Jamie? She wanted to hurt Jamie in return.

"Takes one to know one."

"Have we just returned to kindergarten?" Poppy wanted to hate this fashionably gorgeous model, except she saw the hurt under her sharp exterior. Pity was all she felt.

"Fuck you. If you were prettier, you'd be a real threat. I'm done wasting my breath on you." Wow, Jamie sure had a way of hitting a sore spot. Bile rose in the back of Poppy's throat as the tiny ball of sympathy fled. She needed to sit down. Jamie pushed past her, barging her with her shoulder, and Poppy staggered sideways a step. She twisted to watch her stalk away, her own breath shallow. After a moment, Poppy walked to the toilets and stared at the handprint outlined on her cheek. No amount of makeup would hide that. Maybe it would fade in a few minutes. Or maybe she should just go home. The slap only added to the sense that she didn't belong in this glamourous world of Stu's career. Although why should she let a rude bitch ruin her evening? Poppy rubbed both her cheeks and pulled out her phone. She thumbed through her social media for a while until her cheek stopped hurting. With a quick glance in the mirror to check her face, Poppy walked back into the main room. She brushed down her dress as she stepped around groups of people chatting. Until the incredibly confusing discussion with Jamie, the rest of the evening had been fairly dull. Perhaps if she made more effort to join the conversations, it wouldn't be so snore-inducing. Or hopefully, now the awards were all given out, and people's tongues were freed up, the topics would broaden away from each person talking themselves up. Poppy realised she'd been staring at the floor as she minced her way past each noisy group. She looked up.

Stu stood beside his table, his arm slung casually over Jamie's shoulders. Poppy's heart stopped. She didn't belong in this world. She didn't understand how Stu could be so goddamned fucking casual with an ex-lover who slapped her. Unless she wasn't an ex. This couldn't be happening again. With her face stinging and tight heat throbbing behind her eyes, Poppy spun around and ran from the room. Once outside, she dug into her purse, pulled out her phone and ordered a cab. All she wanted was to get home, rip off this stupid gown, and cuddle Dread. The loudest voice in her head was named Doubt, and he sang with a million reasons why she shouldn't, couldn't stay. Would Stu even notice her absence? Jean-Phillipe hadn't.

16

Poppy stood in her kitchen, eating breakfast, purely for something to do. She didn't particularly want to eat. She hadn't slept much last night. Her phone had pinged several times with messages from Stu asking if she was okay. She'd eventually replied with a short yeah, just to shut him up. It did nothing to quiet the voice in her head and she'd spent too many hours awake berating herself for believing Stu was different to Jean-Phillipe. Stu was kind, where Jean-Phillipe had focused on fixing her supposed flaws. Poppy grimaced. Why had she tricked herself into thinking Stu accepted, even appreciated, her unfashionable body and her creative outlook on life? For fuck's sake, he was creative himself. He should get it. But then, so was Jean-Phillipe, and look how well that had turned out. Or maybe she shouldn't paint them both with the same tarred brush? She shoved a spoonful of cereal in her mouth, focusing on chewing to try and stop the cycle of negative thoughts rampaging in her head. Her phone rang. Stu. Should she give him a chance to explain? Probably.

"Yeah?" She swallowed her mouthful.

"How are you this morning? Did you get your dress fixed?"

"My dress?" Poppy placed the spoon back in the bowl.

"Jamie told me you had an issue with your dress, and you had to leave."

Poppy snorted. Yeah, that wasn't the truth at all. If Stu believed that, he was a bigger fool than her.

He blithely continued. "She said you'd asked her to tell me you had to go home to fix it." As if that justified his actions. Only in a world without phones would it make sense for her to leave a message with his ex. Didn't he think she might have called if it was that simple? Obviously, he didn't think she was worth the basic courtesy of common sense. It might have been nice if he'd called for her opinion on the matter, rather than listen to his poisonous ex. She dismissed the notion of unfairness; he had tried by sending a million texts, and she'd ignored him. Well, it didn't mean she would roll over and pretend it was okay for him to hug someone who'd just slapped her. Poppy valued herself higher than this throwaway view he had of her.

"Tell me more about Jamie and how she gets to decide if I'm okay."

Stu huffed in her ear, a blokey version of an exasperated sigh. "I know Jamie can be tricky at times. Her father, Cleveland, is an arse, and one of our main rivals at Kapow."

"Okay." Poppy didn't even try to begin to understand

why he'd want to be pals with his rival's daughter. Let alone have a relationship with her. What a mess.

"But she's alright once you get to know her."

"Uh, huh." Poppy rolled her eyes. Spoken like a bloke. She didn't want any part of getting to know Jamie better. She knew plenty enough already.

"She said you told her to pass on the message that I should stay and enjoy myself."

"Right. And you chose to believe her?" Poppy couldn't believe the audacity of his statement. He believed a fucking society blogger over her. So much for her opinion mattering.

"Well, I sent you a few texts and you didn't reply until after midnight."

Poppy ground her teeth. "Because I'm not the fucking fairy god mother. Your cute society fuck buddy slapped me. That's why I left."

"Fuck buddy. Are you serious? Is this whole thing a big fucking joke to you? First the arse appreciation comment in front of my colleagues and now this. You have to be—"

Poppy hung up. Her whole body shook with tension, her palms clammy, and her temples ached from the rigidity in her muscles. How dare he! How dare he have the fucking balls to blame her for this mess? If he couldn't tell her the truth, she didn't want any part of a world where lies were standard. Advertising. She should have known better. She shouldn't have trusted him. Her hands shook as she stared at the ceiling. Thank Zeus, she'd managed to keep an emotional distance. Because she'd been here before, she'd kept her heart safe. The sex had been great, wonderful, thrilling…. Finished. She sank to the floor, eyes closed. Her phone rang again, and she let it ring out. Eventually, it beeped with a message notification.

Dread slunk over and rubbed against her. She reached out for him, and he leapt into her lap and started to purr. The cat's happy vibrations did nothing to ease the shards of pain piercing her lungs. Shit. Hot tears formed in her eyes, and she dashed them away with the back of her hand. Guard her heart. Who was she kidding? Only herself. This ache could only come because she'd been silly enough to believe the idea that lust and sexual chemistry equated to love. Just because their bodies connected, and sizzled, didn't mean it meant anything. Obviously it meant nothing to him if he could cuddle up to his ex in public, and not even care when he heard her say Jamie had slapped her. All he cared about was his image, and how bad she'd made him look with her awkward slip of the tongue. As if she didn't regret Levi's fucking stupid joke enough. She pressed her fist against her heart. Damn it. She had to go to work. Levi would want all the gossip from the awards night. She swallowed and sat up straight. She was tough. She could do this. She'd survived betrayal once before. She could do it again. Poppy sniffed before shifting Dread off her lap.

"Sorry Dread, I have to go to work. Try not to bring any dead crickets inside today. I don't think I'll have the heart to clean them up tonight." Tonight, she'd lose herself in one of her favourite movies. She couldn't stomach a love story right now. Not with her own heart smashed into smithereens under Stu's giant feet. She wanted a completely escapist and brutal movie to drown in. Maybe something angsty and ridiculous, a film to indulge this feeling of foolishness. She sucked in a tight breath. First, she had to get through the day. She staggered to her feet, her eyes blurry, and went through the motions of getting ready for another day at work.

"How was the party?" Levi grinned as he arrived at work. Poppy glanced up at her apprentice, then went back to the tedious task of organising drawers. How long had it been since she did this? She threw old empty packets into a bin. Her habit of flinging rubbish into drawers as she worked created this mess. Today, it felt cathartic to biff stuff away.

"Yeah, alright."

"Judging by your hangover eyes, I'd hazard a guess that you had a bloody marvellous time. Must feel pretty good to walk on Stu's arm with everyone staring at his arse."

"You and your—" Poppy swallowed back the curse. "— damned joke about the Stu Arse Appreciation Society. I'm pretty sure no-one was looking at Stu when we arrived." Poppy rubbed her hands together. That goddamned joke.

"What? They all stared at your fantastic hair?" Levi laughed, and tossed his fringe back off his face.

"Ha. No. Unless it was to gawk at the only person with brightly coloured hair."

Sympathy flashed over Levi's face. "Whatever. I've read the society pages. Nearly all of them have fake blonde hair."

Poppy blew out a short breath. Yeah, just like back-stabbing Jamie, all prettied up by Jean-Phillipe, in a move which felt like a giant 'get fucked'.

She swallowed. "Probably. No, most people weren't staring at Stu, they were staring at his boss. Now there is an arse for your little one man society." Even she could hear the bravado in her voice.

"Oh. Tell me." Levi grinned and wiggled his fingers. He didn't seem to hear the lie in her tone.

"Stu's boss, Vince. He's the ultimate bad boy rich guy, you know the type that only exists in novels and rom com movies. Every eye was glued to him. Stu and I—" Poppy cringed at her own phrasing. "Well, we didn't rate much of a look from the cameras."

"And the party. I'm guessing there was plenty of champagne."

Poppy forced a smile. "Much needed champagne. I've never sat through such a long drawn out evening of self-congratulation. You wouldn't believe how many awards they gave out."

"You get an award. You can an award. Hell, everyone gets an award." Levi waved his arms flamboyantly.

"Pretty much. It became quite ridiculous."

"Speaking of everyone getting an award, your sexy Stu is here."

Poppy spun towards the door as Stu walked in. His glorious body, one she'd run her hands all over, moved with confident ease. He wore simple blue jeans, and a green t-shirt. The casual clothes only emphasized his strength and made his blue eyes glow as he stared at her.

"Poppy." He breathed out her name, and his voice rumbled inside her. Warm. Familiar. She almost forgot she was mad at him. "Jamie is sorry that she slapped you. I've told her it was out of line and she should apologise in person."

Poppy wanted to stomp her foot and squeal. He wouldn't believe her, but he'd believe Jamie. "It's not appropriate for you to come to my work place and have this discussion." Poppy kept her voice flat when all she wanted to do was hurl insults at him and chase him out of her shop. This was her place. How dare he barge in here with his crappy fake apology?

"I'll mind the shop, if you want to go out for a chat." Levi's sing song tones filled the tense silence.

"Nope. I'm not going anywhere." Poppy couldn't argue with him. Not when her heart was already in pieces. Hot tears burned her eyes. She would not cry in front of him. She blinked once and stared at him with the rudest glare she could summon. He raised his eyebrows and pounced, sweeping her into his arms and storming to the back cupboard.

"I'll mind the shop. I promise not to swoon." Levi called out as Stu pushed open the door. He slammed it behind him. Dark surrounded Poppy, and she reached out for the light switch.

"Fuck you." Poppy spat out as he caught her hand.

"Why? I'm trying to help."

"Some fucking help this is. First you believe your shitty ex over me, and now you've kidnapped me in the storeroom of my own business. Nope, I'm out."

"Ok, I'll grant you that this isn't my most rational of moments."

"I think that's the first true thing you've said to me. Is everything you do as fake as your hair?"

"Tell me what you really think, Poppy." Was that hurt

she heard in his voice? No, that would mean he cared about her. It couldn't be. His actions didn't line up…

"What I really think?"

"Yes."

"Can I turn the light on?"

"No."

"Why the fuck not? This is my business. My shop. You don't get to dictate terms." She tried to wipe away the tears streaming down her face, but he held her hand tight.

"Yes I do. You are in the wrong here. You can't come to my work function, and embarrass me in front of my colleagues. Do you know how many texts I've had today saying 'nice arse'?"

Poppy choked on a shocked laugh as a million emotions flooded her body. Rage being the biggest one.

"She slapped me. If you'd just turn on the light, you'll see her fucking fingerprints bruised on my face. Not a little tickle of a cat fight, Stu. A proper full blown slap." Poppy dragged in a sharp breath as Stu gasped. "And. And you fucking have the poor sense to believe her and not me. How dare you?"

"I…"

"No. Stu. You don't get to say anything. Saying something awkward doesn't equate at all to being slapped. You are not hard done by here. It's only your ego and image that cares about what your friends think of you. If they tease you about some chick liking your arse, that can only be good for you. There is no good in being chased by a crazy ex and being slogged in the face."

"What did you say to her?"

"That's not the right question, Stu. Maybe you should be on my fucking side and ask what bullshit she said to me. Whining about how it's not fair because I look like your bloody favourite painting. Oh, and how it's not fair that you dumped her because she accidentally on purpose kissed your boss."

"Stop. She never kissed Vince. He's… not like that."

"But she is?"

"No. We didn't break up because of Vince. We broke up because it wasn't fair on her. I thought we were just having some fun and she was under pressure from her father to make it more. She's a good friend in a complicated situation, Poppy, and I won't pit you against each other."

"You have to pick a side. And it's pretty damned clear to me that you've picked her. So go on with you." Poppy was glad of the dark, as it hid the tears streaming down her face. She leaned against the shelf, hard against her back, and sniffed. Stu's citrusy scent filled the whole space. The cupboard should have smelled like bleach and hair product, not the welcoming scent of Stu's body up close. Poppy scrubbed away the tears with the back of her hand. She thumped him on the chest to get him away from her.

"It's not that simple. Please. Let me explain." Stu's voice sounded as ragged as she felt, rung out like a piece of road kill run over by a hundred trucks. Poppy's ears filled with sound of red hot blood raging.

"You don't get to have me. Get out." Her chest heaved with ragged breaths, echoing against the pain in her head and her heart. Stu shifted in the dark, and she started to sag with the expectation that he was leaving. Instead, he leaned closer, his body too near and her skin prickled all over. He kissed her lightly on the forehead, then light streamed in for a second as he walked away. Gone. The cupboard door closed with an unsatisfying click, when all she wanted was a decent slam. She sagged to the floor in the dark and let the tears come in big gulps.

17

"Levi." Stu breathed out as Poppy's apprentice answered the phone. He'd called the salon four times a day for the last two days, wanting to hear Poppy's voice again. He'd walked past more times than could possibly be sane, just to get a glimpse of her. He longed for her, craved her, and couldn't quite understand how it had all gone wrong so fast over a minor misunderstanding. Frustration crept in, surely, Poppy knew how much he cared.

"She doesn't want to talk to you. You have to stop ringing here."

"Don't hang up."

Levi hummed. "Why? You broke the basic tenant of a relationship. Poppy is loyal and caring, and she doesn't deserve you."

"Hang on, what?"

"If you are ringing here to have another go at Poppy because you are butt hurt over a comment she made when nervous, then you are an idiot and you don't get to have her."

"Wow. That's a lot to unwrap there, Levi."

"Not really. You care more about your image than her. In fact, I bet you are calling to make an appointment because you have re-growth. Yeah?"

Stu paused. It had crossed his mind to use that as an excuse to see Poppy again. He swallowed. Maybe he'd misread the situation. Poppy would tell him; she always knew when he'd got caught up in an unrealistic perspective. Fuck. She'd tried to tell him, and he didn't want to listen.

"Good bye Stu. Find another hairdresser, and maybe one day you'll see what you've lost by abusing her trust in you."

"I already know what I've lost, damn you. Everything in my life is cardboard without Poppy."

"Maybe you should have thought about that before you hugged your ex. In public. Right after she'd hit Poppy. I mean, what kind of shithead are you? You can't possibly think that you are in the right here. You've let your big ego put your image ahead of Poppy."

Stu stared out the window as Levi berated him. Deservedly. Butt hurt. Yeah, that described the twang in his heart. He'd been so focused on being successful, to prove a point about his origins, that he'd forgotten what really mattered in life. Success was nothing without love and trust, without family. Image mattered for naught if it covered a paper cut-out version of reality.

"Tell her I'm sorry. I'll make it right." His voice croaked, tight.

"I'm not going to tell her anything."

"Come on, mate, I'm trying to fix this."

"You can't fix this with a few nice words. You'll need to prove that she can depend on you. Stop thinking about yourself and think about her. Imagine if you'd seen her hugging her ex." Levi hung up. Stu paced on his balcony, not seeing the view out over the city. Levi had it wrong. All he'd thought about for the last forty-eight hours was Poppy. Damn it, she'd dominated his thoughts for the past two years, until he'd taken the first step to make his longings real. Levi's comment rattled around. *"You've put your ego ahead of Poppy."* He sucked in a deep breath and leaned on the railing. His heart clenched, pain enveloping him. *"Imagine if you'd seen her hugging her ex."* He hung his head, finally acknowledging the one thing he'd refused to contemplate. He loved Poppy. Deeply loved her. And he'd hurt her by not putting her first in his life. He'd fucked it all up. He had to fix this.

"What are you doing here?" The caution, and defiance, in Poppy's voice made Stu cringe. He'd waited on the steps of her apartment for hours for her to come home.

"I just came to say I'm sorry. I really messed up by putting my ego and my complicated friendship with Jamie before you. I believed Jamie and I forgot that she's under a lot of pressure to do what her father tells her, so she makes bad choices."

"I don't want to hear about her."

"You're right. I'm sorry I put my image first. I'm sorry I didn't notice you were nervous, and I'm sorry I didn't give Jamie some notice before she met you so she could have time to adjust."

"Adjust?"

"I'm sorry. I really am, truly and deeply sorry about the whole mess. I've brought you a little gift." Stu handed over a shiny red wrapped box with a giant black ribbon on top. The wind caught Poppy's hair, sending long strands buffeting around her face. The wrapping paper and ribbon matched her current hair colour. He hadn't noticed his choice until now as he stood, hopeful, before her. Of all the wildly creative ideas he'd had in his career, this one took the gold medal as the most risky. This could easily backfire on him, and yet, he hoped, it was precisely this risk that would demonstrate how much he cared. The whole point of his choice was to show Poppy how far he'd go for her. She glared at him, then flicked her gaze down at the present.

"Go on, open it." He pleaded, and she tugged the ribbon to unravel it and tore at the paper. Stu held his breath as she lifted the lid on the box.

"A butt plug?"

"Surprise!" Stu grinned despite the churn in his gut and the dryness in his mouth.

"No-one wants a surprise butt plug." Poppy blinked slowly.

"It's a symbol of trust."

Poppy sighed and shook her head, a long suffering type of sigh, and his heart stopped beating. "You don't get it, do you? If I tell you I don't trust you, you don't give me a gift that basically requires me to trust you more."

"No. No. You have it backwards." He waved his hands, frantic. "I want you to try it on me, if you want, because I want to gift you power over me. I trust you to treat me with care," Stu implored. She had more power over him than she could possibly understand.

"Oh." Poppy stared, open-eyed. She tilted her head, considering. He hoped the emotion flashing in her eyes was hunger and need. Either that, or he'd totally screwed up and she wanted to get the fuck away from him.

"Plus, if you say yes, there is another gift underneath." Stu's chest tightened, his pulse hammering as her eyes narrowed.

"I hope it's not a pair of butt plugs, because while one might be quirky, two is down-right freaking weird."

Stu smothered his own mouth with his hand as he laughed. "Ahh, Poppy, I've missed you." He took a step closer to her. She half-stepped backwards and held up her palm, so he stopped.

"Not yet." She picked up the butt plug and peered into the box. Stu held his breath.

"Paris?"

"The city of love." *For you, Poppy, my love.* The words dried on his tongue, unable to get them out at the crucial moment. The cagey look on her face made him halt. No matter how much his guts hurt, and his chest ached, and how much he wanted to tell her, he wouldn't be the guy who manipulated and cajoled a woman to do his bidding. He wanted to her choose to come with him, without pressure. Free and trusting.

"And what about the salon? And Dread?"

"The salon can shut for two weeks for renovations. I have everything in place, and your Mama will look after Dread." He loved the way her family rallied around the make things happen for her, a wonderful support network which he wanted to be part of.

"You talked to Mama about taking me to Paris." Poppy's eyebrows shot up.

"Look, I know it was a little presumptuous of me—"

"Sure was. Did you tell her how you expect me to be friends with all your ex's, even the ones that slap me?" Her bottom lip curled up. "And don't say I didn't tell you. I did. You just went on and on about her hard-done life as a fucking trust fund kid with millions of dollars and no need to work to survive."

"Money doesn't matter when your dad bashes you. She hit you because that's what she's been taught. She's truly sorry. But you know what, this isn't about Jamie. I should have listened to you. I fucked up, Poppy."

"You sure did." Poppy's breasts heaved as she took another step backward. "Shit. I'm sorry to hear that about Jamie. That sucks." Her eyes darted around as she hauled in a deep breath. He held his, waiting for her.

"It does. I still shouldn't have put her needs above yours."

Poppy sighed. "I wish you'd told me about her before the awards dinner. I wouldn't have been so abrupt with her when we argued. You know what, how about we get her involved with the re-launch of Spiro's? It might be nice for her…" She tugged on the end of her ponytail, her eyebrows drawn together. Stu wanted to pull her into a hard hug. The warning on her face stopped him cold. He reached up and gently brushed his finger over the deep wrinkle between her eyes.

"Ahh, my Poppy. You have the biggest heart." *And I fucking love you.* He almost said it aloud, only her hesitance made the words die on his tongue again. He almost covered up his racing heart with an awkward comment about how big Jamie's social network was and how good that would be for publicity, but managed to stop himself. Praising her wasn't the best timing, not when Poppy had almost said yes to the one thing Stu wanted most of all.

"Um, thanks." The breeze picked up stray tendrils of her hair loosened from her ponytail, and he tucked them behind her ear. Tender warmth built in his lungs, as they stood close together, almost touching with his gift as a barrier between them. His arm muscles shook with the effort of standing still and respecting her space while his whole body buzzed with her nearness.

"Come to Paris with me." He rasped, his voice rough and needy. "I want to show you my favourite paintings. I want to worship you in the city of love. Two weeks, and while we are away, your brother is going to manage the re-fit of Spiros."

"Holy fuck, Stu. Have you told my whole family?" Her frown disappeared as she raised her eyebrows.

"No. Not all of them. Bloody hell, do you know how much family you have? I haven't had time to tell them all."

She laughed. "You told Mama and Christos. Therefore, they all know." Her throaty laughter washed over his skin giving him goose bumps of anticipation.

"Then you'd better say yes. You know you can't disappoint them."

Poppy slapped him on the chest and rolled her eyes. "Paris and an incredibly different gift of trust, you know I was always going to say yes to that!"

Stu's breath raced out on a long breath of relief. "Can I seal your agreement with a kiss?"

"Yes." She stretched up and touched her lips to his. Heat seared him. Poppy tasted of home, sweet and tart and so goddamned perfect.

18

Poppy couldn't get her original fantasy out of her brain. The idea of Stu stretched out on her bed, his hands tied to the bedhead in black silk, his muscles taut as she teased him. Throw in his gift, and she could play with him until he begged her for release. She squirmed in the business class seat, her underwear damp. For her own sanity, she'd refused to let him stay the night after his gift and incendiary kiss. She shouldn't have agreed to the kiss. The familiar taste of Stu made her long for him. She wanted to crush the little doubt inside and trust him. But could she trust him, really trust him, when it mattered? Poppy still wanted space to decide, and after another night alone she was sure her heart couldn't cope with another leap of trust. He hadn't answered the question about whether she belonged in his life. He acted like she should blithely comply with him without the need for him to declare his feelings. Hadn't he? She was so confused by his initial reaction and then his apology. The two things seemed to be at odds with each other and she didn't know which one was real.

Perhaps if he'd said he loved her? Then she might be willing to let herself the freedom to acknowledge her love for him. Right now, she had to keep her distance, because he did too. How long would they both circle around the idea, each of them not wanting to go first? Well, he would have to be first, because tickets to Paris might be fancy, but she wouldn't be won by money or romance. She'd be won by the truth.

To complicate matters, the family grapevine buzzed with the news. He'd only given her two days to pack—thankfully she had a valid passport—and there was plenty to organise. Poppy had spent the time racing around, grateful she'd been too busy to worry about the trip. She had to approve the changes to the salon, buy winter clothes for Paris in early November (a virtually impossible task in Sydney as summer stock filled all the shelves), and most importantly, take the time to introduce Mama to Dread. The last item on her preparation list was the one that caused all the drama. Stu asked Mama to look after Dread, and as soon as Mama mentioned it to one of her sisters, everyone knew, and they all rang to congratulate her.

The family started organising her wedding—a proper Greek extravaganza—and Poppy didn't have the heart to tell them it was too soon. She'd agreed to go to Paris and be wooed by Stu, not to be bound to him forever. If only her heart didn't leap at the prospect, or swoon at the way the family gathered around at his command to do the upgrades on her salon. He'd even managed to cosy up to Aunt Maria.

Initially she'd been annoyed that he'd gone to her family before telling her about his plans for Paris. The irritation quickly subsided when he used his own special brand of charm to convince the family that the changes she wanted were the best for everyone.

In any other circumstance, the idea of going to Paris with her lover would have her dragging him into the ridiculously tiny airplane toilet to join the mile high club. The thought was surreal, even the idea of this flight to the city of love, if only she could banish the tiny fragment of doubt overshadowing the whole thing. Why her? He'd done everything possible to prove he wanted her, and her family accepted and welcomed him, except for the one thing she wanted; him to show he truly loved her. The awards night kept all the nagging doubts forefront in her mind. The connection between them felt fragile, as if it was stretched thin by his actions, ready to break if he didn't listen to her again. She wasn't ready to rebuild the connection just yet… Or was she? If not, why was she in this plane? The captain announced they would be landing in the next half hour, and Poppy glanced over at Stu.

He put down his laptop and twisted in his seat. "About Jamie…"

"I don't want to know about your ex. I don't care that her dad is an arsehole. I mean, I do care about that because it's a shit situation and I wouldn't wish it on anyone. But shit, Stu, I didn't agree to fly to the other side of the world to hear a sob story about her." Poppy clenched her teeth. All fantasies fled, and she glared at him. What a way to begin their adventure together.

"Okay. I get it. It's not what I was going to say."

"Then what?" She hurled the words at him, almost hissing.

"I broke up with her nearly two years ago when I found her hugging Vince."

"I know. I accused her of dumping you to upgrade with your boss."

Stu nodded. "It's an easy assumption to make. I did the same and later when I found out the truth, we became friends again, but at the time I was hurt..."

"She hurt your fragile ego." Poppy sneered. It was so tempting to want to hurt him as he'd hurt her. She stared out the window at the mist as they descended through the clouds, and her stomach flipped and twisted.

"Poppy, have I told you how good you are for me? Yes, she hurt my ego, but she also hurt me. If I couldn't trust my partner, who could I trust?"

"Jinx." She muttered under her breath. Did this mean he actually understood?

"Yes! That's what I've realised. I am the shithead Levi said I was. I did exactly the same thing to you, and I'm so sorry."

"Levi said that? Ha, I've trained him well." She couldn't resist turning towards him, and she bit the inside of her cheek as a grin threatened to break out. Poor Stu, he appeared mystified by her response to his apology.

"He's exceeded the bounds of loyalty to you."

"Has he now? How exactly?" Poppy sniffed. "No, scratch that. Because he told you an uncomfortable truth and you didn't want to hear it. You can't hide that with fancy words."

Stu nodded. "I can never hide from you, even when I want you. I adore the way you are so grounded, rational, and you say just the thing I don't want to hear."

"Stop. You don't need to flatter me."

"It's not flattery. I need someone in my life who will tell me the truth. Someone who will stop me getting too self-important."

"And you think that person is me?" Poppy couldn't hold back the incredulous tone. Blood pulsed around her body, her emotions in disarray.

"Yes! You are the only person in my life who does that for me. Mum thinks I'm her greatest achievement, and Vince, who I trust with my life, often says whatever it takes to keep the focus on the business. No-one else matters that much, so they are easy to dismiss. You matter, and you see through me."

"Sounds uncomfortable." Snark coloured her tone as she tried to keep her distance from him. She mattered to him. Her heart thumped helplessly, wishing it was the declaration of love she wanted. Shit. She'd already forgiven him because she loved him and she wanted—more than anything—for him to love her back. She didn't care about Paris, or his gifts of forgiveness, she wanted to be loved for exactly who she was, a hairdresser whose self-doubt clashed with her ambition.

"Yes! Yes, it is. That's basically why I acted badly at the Awards Dinner. Everyone spent all night telling me how great I am, and there you were, seeing that it was all bullshit. I didn't want to listen to reality, and I'm sorry." Stu twisted in his seat, imploring her with his intense gaze.

Poppy swallowed down the pointless hope that flared in the back of her throat. "You are asking a big burden of me."

"How so?"

"To be your truth-teller when you don't want to listen. You are essentially asking me to have the emotional burden of always being the bad guy. It's a big ask."

"You think I should be able to do this for myself?"

"That'd be sensible. Preferable, even." Poppy raised her eyebrows. Stu opened his mouth to speak, and she lifted a finger to his lips to stop him. Heat seared her finger, slamming up her arm and reverberating in her chest.

"Don't say it. Don't say 'that's why I need you, because you always talk sense to me'. Learn how to talk sense to yourself." Poppy knew she was being slightly bitchy, but she couldn't work out any other way to make him see the burden he placed on her. Why should it be up to her to make him see his own errors? And what would happen when he tired of her always being the negative voice in his life? Because the gap between reality and negativity was short one when he lived in the land of continuous praise. She was saved from any further comment by the final landing comment from the flight attendants over the intercom.

A couple of hours later, they'd cleared customs and caught a taxi into the heart of Paris. Poppy had listened to Stu's rambling chatter about their surroundings, and his previous trips to Paris. The closest she'd been to Paris were two family trips to Greece; one when she was ten, and one when she was sixteen. Europe was a long way from Australia, a long expensive trip.

"Where to first?" Stu held out his hand as he opened the door of the taxi. The confronting smell of cigarette smoke gave Poppy a start. Not at all what she expected from the city of love. Flowers, cupcakes, sultry red wine, and pastry, perhaps. Did everyone smoke here? So different to Australia, where hardly anyone smoked anymore.

"Is this our hotel? I'd love to have a shower and get changed." Poppy stared up at the ancient white stone building with intricate carved window frames. The light here was softer than at home, and she couldn't work out what time of day it was.

"Good plan. Then we can grab a late lunch and go for a walk along the Seine. Unless you want to do something different. The Musee d'Orsay is only a block away, and I'd love to show you some of my favourite paintings." Stu shrugged one shoulder, then turned to grab their luggage from the taxi driver. Poppy stood helplessly in the street, staring at the flash of vulnerability in his eyes. He always made it her choice, never railroaded her into anything. Even when he really wanted something—like now?—he waited for her to decide. How could she be so blind? He didn't doubt her. He didn't control her. He gifted her with the power of choice, and she was letting her insecurities and her past experiences with handsome men hold them both back.

"Stu?" She should tell him now. *I love you. We can make this work.* But the words stuck in her throat as he stood in the Parisian street with his dark hair contrasting to the old stone. His fake silver fox had re-growth, so even his temples were darker than she'd become used to. He belonged here in this beautiful city. Hints of jasmine floated past, mingling with the pungent city smells. The taxi drove off with a roar.

"Yeah?"

"Let's get inside." She had to tell him about Jean-Phillipe, to banish him to her past forever. She needed to move forward and embrace the future. With Stu. Her toes tapped in her shoe as Stu checked them into the hotel. He spoke French to the attendant, the romantic language swirling around Poppy in his rich voice. She combed her hands through her hair, twisting the long red and black strands out of habit. Eventually, they followed the concierge to their room.

"What is the urgency, Poppy?" Stu shut the door and turned to face her.

"It's not urgent. Do you want to shower first?" Suddenly all the travel grit clung to her skin and she wanted to clear her head before she talked about this.

"No, you go first. I'll sort out our luggage."

Poppy nodded and fled to the shower. The hot water on her skin was so good and refreshing. Her mind cleared as she turned off the water and towelled herself dry. She stepped out of the bathroom to see Stu making tea for her.

"Here. Drink this while I shower, and then we can work out what to do."

Poppy clutched the towel against her body as his gaze swept over her, then he walked past her with a gentle brush of his fingers across her shoulder.

"I'll be back soon." True to his word, she only had time to get dressed, run her fingers through her damp hair, and sip the now cool tea, before he walked out of the bathroom with a towel around his waist. His hair was damp, slightly curly at the ends, and he smiled at her. She sucked in a short breath and began before she could doubt herself.

"When I was eighteen, I made a terrible choice, and it's still haunting me." She wiped her clammy palms on her jeans.

"It's okay." Stu stepped forward and embraced her, his hands gently holding her face.

"No, it's not. At first, I was so flattered. I gained an apprenticeship at the best salon in Sydney, and the owner smothered me with attention. God, I was so naïve. I thought I was so special. I believed his promises."

"He abused you?" The muscles in Stu's face tightened, and he dropped his hands away from her face.

"No. I agreed to sleep with him. I was young and foolish, and I believed him when he told me glorious things about myself. I wanted to believe him, and I thought if I slept with him, his words would become true. It was only later that I found out it was all a lie. I arrived at his apartment after my shift one afternoon and found him in bed with another apprentice. I wasn't special. He fucked all his apprentices, made us all the same promises." She hated the way her stomach fell at the memory. Even after all this time, Jean-Pierre had built her up, then ripped it all away, and she'd never truly believed in herself since.

"That fucker." Stu paced around the room, his hands balled into tight fists. Angry energy poured off him. For her. Her doubts about him fled. She wanted to taste him, to have all his righteous fury on her tongue, because he was mad on her behalf. For her.

"It doesn't matter anymore. I learnt not to trust handsome men." Poppy whispered. She didn't want to acknowledge how the experience shaped her view of Stu. The unfairness of her grouping Stu with a dickhead like Jean-Phillipe made her cross her arms and hug herself tight. She had to acknowledge her role here if she was going to move forward and embrace life. The risk of his rejection was worth it to send doubt to the end of the earth and open herself up to him.

Stu's eyes flashed, dark blue and intense, as he stopped pacing to stand only a step away from her. "And when you saw me with Jamie, you saw him."

"Yeah. I'm sorry." Poppy hung her head. "You aren't like him at all."

"Except I didn't listen. I hurt you. I'm amazed you agreed to come with me at all."

Poppy looked up. Stu stared at her with such intensity, and so much heat, as if she stared at an explosion up close. All that searing connection, aimed at her. The time had arrived. To claim him.

"Stu. I love you, that's why I came to Paris with you."

He fell to his knees before her, his breath releasing in a hot wind across her skin. "Thank fuck. Oh my God, Poppy, I've wanted you for so long. And as soon as I touched you, I knew I'd give you the world to hear you say that. I love you."

She dragged her fingers through his hair, perfect strands against her fingertips. The depth of desire in his gaze, the raw hunger, made her knees tremble.

"Get up. Come with me." She dug her fingers into the back of his skull and he rose to his feet. Her nipples hardened as his body dragged up against hers. He towered over her, but his size made her feel safe, especially with his declaration of love still on his lips. He wrapped his arms around her waist and started to lift her up.

"No, put me down. I want…"

He relaxed his hold. "I hope you want what I want."

"Well—" She flicked her head, so her hair grazed his cheek. Colour slashed across his face and desire pooled in her stomach. A reward.

"Yes, please. Do that again." Gravel made his voice low, a sexy rumble which created a fresh dampness between her thighs.

"Only if you do as I say."

"Poppy. Fuck, I love it when you talk to me like that." Stu's mouth parted, and she couldn't resist brushing her lips against his. He slid his hand up her back, cradling her head, his fingers threaded in her hair, and her knees softened as he deepened the kiss. She felt herself falling under his spell, and she dragged herself out of the passionate mist before her brain gave up all command.

"Get nude." She couldn't form more words than the bare minimum.

"For you, anything." Stu tugged at the towel and it fell to the ground. She reached out for the sprinkling of chest hair, spreading her fingers through the short strands, and over his strong muscles. His chest rose and fell as she explored the familiar shape, and his citrusy salty smell filled her nostrils. She wanted to bite his nipple, to see him gasp.

Later. Soon. He stood before her in all his naked glory. This man, this perfect specimen of a man, was hers to command. And judging by the size of his erection, he wanted her to do it. She swallowed, her mouth flooding with moisture as she processed the implication. He wanted her. She traced her finger, impossibly lightly, up his cock. She wanted to drink his groan. And she would soon.

"Come." She turned away from him, her hand behind her, still touching the end of his cock. Walking towards the hotel suite's bedroom, he followed at the perfect pace to keep the connection between them. Even though all she did was hold her hand behind her as she walked, it felt like she led him, like she enforced the faint connection between her and him. The bed, a massive four poster like something from a historical movie, dominated the room.

"Lie down."

"Face up or face down?" His question made her suck in a sharp breath. Heat pulsed inside her at the possibilities.

"Face up." Her voice cracked. "And spread your arms and legs." He complied; a naked god spreadeagled for her. She had to clench her legs together at the surge of wet heat. Now, the next step…

"Stay." She left the room to grab a few supplies from her luggage, silk ties that she'd packed in hope, not expecting to use them so soon. Stu's face relaxed as she returned to the room, the slow ease of breath he released making her smile.

"Did you think I'd abandon you?"

He cleared his throat, her attention torn to the way his throat shifted.

"Poor darling. I'd never be that cruel." She leaned over

and pressed a hot kiss to the hollow at the base of his neck. With the black silk ties, she looped one around his wrist, enjoying the way goose flesh broke out on his arms as she touched him. She deliberately kept her gaze away from his glorious cock, to prolong the anticipation. Poppy wanted to suck him. Deep and hard. But not until he begged for it. She rounded the bed to tie his other hand to the other post.

"Tie me tighter. Take control, Poppy. It's yours if you want it." His nostrils flared as his voice rumbled. She smiled.

"I trust you not to move."

He growled in response, as she traced a circle on his palm. His fingers tried to close over hers, and she shook her head.

"No, Stu. No moving." She traced her hand along the inside of his arm, over each muscle, down the softer more sensitive skin near his armpit.

"Hell, Poppy." His stomach muscles clenched, each strong indent more apparent.

"Are you ticklish?" She breathed on his skin, almost close enough for a kiss. He shifted towards her slightly, and she stood up. She walked to the end of the bed and considered him.

"No moving or I stop. Not unless I say you can." How long could she play with him until he begged to touch her? She ran her hands through her hair and let it fall around her shoulders. He didn't react. Good. She pulled off her fresh shirt and flung it to the corner of the room. The shower had washed away the flight and now anticipation overtook any tiredness from their flight; sleep could come later and if she had her way, they'd both be properly exhausted. Only the rustle of silk gave any sign that he'd noticed. She placed her foot on the end of the bed to remove her sock, then repeated with the other one. His stare never left hers, unblinking with longing. She sat on the end of the bed, facing away from him, and leaned backwards to tug off her jeans. He hissed as her hair fell over his cock. Perfect. Rid of her jeans, she swung around slowly, tracing his thigh with her hair.

"Poppy."

"Yes?"

"You are killing me."

"And I haven't really started." She held his ankles, saw the need in his gaze as she caressed his legs. His black hair rough under her palms, sending sensation up her arms and down into her core. She knelt between his legs, skirting her hands around his cock, not touching him. He twitched as she leaned forward until her breasts hung over his chest. The end of his cock grazed her round stomach. He growled, a low bass to match the thump of her heart. Her underwear was soaked as she pressed her hands on his impressive chest muscles.

"Kiss me. Please."

She bit her lips together to stop the smile of satisfaction as he started to beg. She bent down, bringing her lace covered breasts against him, to press a delicate kiss to his chin. With her arse in the air, and her knees against his balls, his cock throbbed against her stomach. She traced her tongue down his throat, tasting the salt of his sweat as he strained to stay still. Her hair trailed down her back in a long mass, so she grabbed it with one hand and flung it over her shoulder.

"Poppy." He pleaded again as she shifted back on her heels, slowly kissing down his body with her hair spread over his skin, following her kisses. His hips bucked upwards as she blew into his belly button.

"Do you want my lips on you?"

"Yes. Now." Almost the beg she craved. The idea that she could drive him senseless with passion melted her, and sent her so close to the edge, she almost came before she could cover his cock with her lips.

19

S tu loved Poppy. He loved her lush body, he loved her practical outlook on life, and right now, he was freaking in love with her brain. She'd conceived this fantasy, and all his muscles were going to ache tomorrow from holding himself perfectly still for her. Her lips hovered over the end of his cock, as she knelt between his legs. The soft skin of her thighs lightly touching his. Her breath, hot and fast, against the end of his cock.

"Suck me." He begged her to touch him.

"Beg me."

"I am. Please Poppy, let me put my cock in your mouth."

"That's better, Stu." She flashed him a cheeky grin before she slipped her lips over the tip of his cock. Her tongue drew a circle around the end, and he nearly exploded as she sucked him deep. Her hair spread over his stomach, soft, as her lips slid up and down his length. His fingernails dug into his palms. He wanted to pump himself into her, but daren't move. Sex noises filled the room. His groans mixing with her slippery mouth.

"God, Poppy. Let me touch you." He hoped she was wet for him. She changed her angle, and his cock hit the back of her throat. Holy hell.

"Poppy. I have to."

She sucked up his length, her lips leaving him with a little pop, and she glanced at him with heavy eyelids.

"You have to what?"

"I need to be inside you."

She took a long slow breath. "I need that too. I release you from your bonds." He roared as the words left her mouth, wrenching his hands free from her too loose bonds to wrap her in his arms. He kissed her reddened lips, pouring all his tension into her mouth. She took control, sucking his tongue with the same vigour she'd applied to his cock. He picked her up, rolling her underneath him.

"Condom." She whispered. He leapt to his feet, scrambled at her quiet command. At least one of them had some blood left in their brain. He grabbed his wallet, pulled out the foil, and rolled it on himself. She lay on the bed, half sitting resting on her elbows, still encased in lace.

"Can I undress you?"

She smiled, almost a sly knowing smile. "No." Putting on the condom had given him the breather he needed to bring him back from the edge of exploding reason. He stared at her, his pulse galloping.

"No?"

"No. I will do it." She reached behind her back, and her bra pinged loose. With an easy motion, she slid the straps down her arms, and freed her breasts to the air. Her dark rose nipples pebbled in the air as she traced the edge of her breasts with her fingers. He couldn't have looked away if the room was on fire. Fuck it, the room was on fire, so much heat covered his skin. She hooked her fingers under the top of her panties and started to drag them down her legs. Inch by slow inch, she revealed herself to him. She raised up one knee and freed her leg from her underwear.

"Do you like what you see?" Poppy asked, her voice rough as she let her legs fall apart. She was perfect. Pink, soft, wet.

"Yes. I love what I see." He dragged his gaze up towards her face, to look deep into her eyes and show her the truth. "Can I touch you?"

"Not yet." She covered herself with her hand. Pressed two fingers deep inside her. A loud guttural groan filled the air as he grabbed his cock. Her head sagged back as she stroked herself, and he matched her as her moans grew louder.

"Now. Stu. Fuck me now." He didn't need her to say it again. He pounced, slid inside her, and she clenched around him. She came hard and fast, her fingers pressed against her own clit, as he thrust into her. Stars burst behind his eyes and someone called her name over and over. Him. His world began and ended inside her as she gripped him, impossibly tight as another orgasm rippled through her, until he exploded. He collapsed on her, utterly spent, with only enough energy to stroke her hair.

Stu awoke, God knows how much later, cuddled against her back. He had no recollection of them moving position.

She'd dealt with the condom and thrown a blanket over them both.

"Poppy, you are a goddess. My goddess."

She rolled over and kissed him. "Your starving goddess."

"Let's get room service." Stu had no idea what the local time was and he vaguely flung one arm out to see if his phone was in reach.

"Perfect, then you don't have to get dressed."

"I like the way you think. And tomorrow, we can eat baguettes, and I want to show you a painting."

She grinned and kissed him on the nose. "Just one painting?"

"Well, no."

"I knew it. You are going to drag me around a bunch of art galleries, aren't you?"

He shrugged. "It's Paris. Some of the world's greatest art is here. I want to share it with you."

"And if I want to do something different?"

"I'm open to all ideas. Your ideas are excellent." Today proved that. He wanted to hear all her ideas.

She laughed. "Stu, show me art. I want to see the things you love."

"There is one painting I know you will love. Courbet's L'Originie du Monde. Plus, you have to see the Baroque oils. I want to show you the most beautiful women in history. You are the perfect Rubenseque beauty, and I hope you'll understand when you see the nudes. Fashion changes, my heart won't. You'll always be mine."

AUTHOR NOTES

I wrote this book in 2017 when no one had heard of COVID19, and travel for Australians was only limited by a lack of money.

Karahalios is a Greek surname that means bird of prey.

Poppy's cat Dread Pirate George is a nod to The Princess Bride's Dread Pirate Roberts, and is also the online name of the creator of the Silk Road, an underground drug sales website, who was convicted in 2015.

Revani cake recipe:

Ingredients

    1 cup flour

    1 cup fine semolina

    1 tbsp. baking powder

    ½ cup (1 stick) unsalted butter

    1 cup sugar

3 eggs separated

1 tsp. vanilla extract

Zest of 1 lemon

½ tsp orange blossom water

1 cup milk

Pinch of salt

Method

Preheat oven to 350F (xC) and grease a large flat baking pan. Whisk the dry ingredients together (flour, semolina, baking powder). In a separate bowl, cream the butter and sugar until fluffy. Add the egg yolks and keep mixing until yellow, then add the vanilla extract, lemon zest, and orange blossom water. Slowly add the dry ingredients and the milk. In another bowl (yes, there is a bit of cleaning to do afterwards!), beat the egg whites, then fold into your main mixture. Pour into the prepared cake pan, and bake for 45 minutes.

Syrup Ingredients

1½ cups water

1½ cups sugar

Two 3-inch strips of orange zest/peel

1-2 sticks of cinnamon (optional)

1 tsp. freshly squeezed lemon juice

½ tsp orange blossom water

Method

Throw the water, sugar, and orange zest into a pot and

boil. Simmer for a few minutes, then add the lemon juice and orange blossom water. Set aside to cool.

Once the cake is cooked, ladle the syrup evenly over it. If you stab the cake with a fork, the syrup will absorb better. Once cool, cut it up and serve it. You can add almonds to decorate if you are extra fancy!

All Books By Renée Dahlia

Thanks for reading HIS BUXOM BEAUTY. I hope you enjoyed it.

If you'd like to know more about me, my books, or to connect with me online, you can visit my webpage
www.reneedahlia.com
and if you sign up to my newsletter, you can grab a free book *Ode to the Banh Mi*.
Twitter https://twitter.com/dekabat
Facebook https://www.facebook.com/reneedahliawriter/
Instagram
https://www.instagram.com/reneedahlia_author/

Reviews can help readers find books, and I am grateful for all honest reviews. Thank you for taking the time to let others know what you've read, and what you thought.

You've just read a book in my Kapow series. The other books in this series are:

1. Out of Her League (fm with bisexual characters)
1.5 Rekindled (ff) Short Story (also included as a bonus in Out of Her League)
2. His Buxom Beauty (fm)
3. Craving His Spotlight (mm)
4. Her Pregnant Rival (ff)

If you liked this book, here are my other books:

Contemporary Series:

Farrellton Foster Family

1. Betrayed (fm)
2. Liability (ff)
3. Forbidden (fm with bisexual characters)

Merindah Park

1. Merindah Park (fm)
2. Making Her Mark (fm with bisexual heroine)
3. Two Hearts Healing (fm)
4. Racetrack Royalty (fm)

Rainbow Cove

1. His Christmas Pearl (fm)
2. His Christmas Pride Christmas 2020 (mm)

Homage

1. Ode to the Banh Mi (fm with bisexual heroine)
2. Uplift (ff with bisexual heroines): Only One Bed anthology (KU)

***

Historical Series:

Great War Ladies

   1. Her Lady's Honor (ff)

Bluestockings

   0.5 Ten Shipwrecked Books (fm with bisexual hero:
from the 12 Rogues of Christmas anthology, KU)
1. To Charm a Bluestocking (fm with bisexual hero)
2. In Pursuit of a Bluestocking (fm)
3. The Heart of a Bluestocking (fm)